THE
SPORTS
QUIZ
BOOK

Derek O'Brien is an author, a television personality, public speaker, politician and quiz show host.

Born in Kolkata, he began his career as a journalist for *Sportsworld* magazine but soon shifted to advertising. After working for a number of very successful years as Creative Head of Ogilvy, Derek decided to focus all his energy and talent in his passion—quizzing.

Derek is Asia's best-known quizmaster and the CEO of Derek O'Brien & Associates. He was the host of the longest-running game show on Indian television, *The Cadbury Bournvita Quiz Contest*, for which he was voted the Best Anchor of a Game Show at the Indian Television Academy Awards for three years in a row. Always innovating, Derek is also credited with having conducted the first quiz on Twitter in 2010.

He has written over fifty bestselling reference, quiz and school textbooks.

Derek O'Brien is a twice-serving Member of Parliament, elected from West Bengal, and the Parliamentary Party Leader of the All India Trinamool Congress in the Rajya Sabha. He has spoken at, among others, Harvard, Yale and Columbia universities in the US, and several IIMs, IITs and other premier educational institutions in India. He addressed the United Nations General Assembly as a member of the Indian parliamentary delegation in 2012.

Keep in touch with Derek on Twitter, where his handle is @derekobrienmp, and on Facebook at www.facebook.com/derekobrienmp/.

THE
SPORTS
QUIZ
BOOK

DEREK O'BRIEN

RUPA

Published by
Rupa Publications India Pvt. Ltd 2019
7/16, Ansari Road, Daryaganj
New Delhi 110002

Sales Centres:
Allahabad Bengaluru Chennai
Hyderabad Jaipur Kathmandu
Kolkata Mumbai

ISBN: 978-93-5333-621-9

First impression 2019

10 9 8 7 6 5 4 3 2 1

The moral right of the author has been asserted.

CONTENTS

ASHES

1. What is Reginald Shirley Walkinshaw Brooks's contribution to the Ashes?
   a) The name—the Ashes—is said to have originated in a mock obituary written by him.
   b) He coined the term Bodyline.
   c) He compiled the laws of the Ashes.

2. What is the original Ashes Urn made of?
   a) Wood
   b) Terracotta
   c) Glass

3. Who is the only player in the history of the Ashes to be dismissed for handling the ball?
   a) Shane Warne
   b) Graham Gooch
   c) Andrew Flintoff

4. Who has taken the most number of wickets in the Ashes?
   a) Shane Warne
   b) I.T. Botham
   c) Glenn McGrath

5. The 1998-99 Ashes series saw the introduction of...
   a) An actual trophy
   b) Floodlights
   c) Wickets with microphones

6. The *Duckworth Lewis Method* is an album full of songs inspired by cricket. The track 'Jiggery Pokery' from the album is inspired by which incident?
    a) Andrew Strauss's slip catch at Trent Bridge in 2005
    b) Andrew Flintoff's five-wicket haul in 2009
    c) Shane Warne's first delivery in Ashes in 1993

7. Which fielder has taken the most number of catches in the history of the Ashes?
    a) Shane Warne
    b) Glenn McGrath
    c) Ian Botham

8. Which cricketer co-wrote the book *In Quest of the Ashes*?
    a) Ian Chappell
    b) Douglas Jardine
    c) Ricky Ponting

9. After the death of Ivo Bligh, captain of the English team during the 1882-83 tour to Australia, which cricket club received the Ashes Urn from his wife?
    a) Melbourne Cricket Club
    b) Marylebone Cricket Club
    c) Lancashire Cricket Club

10. The record for the most runs by a player in the Ashes has stood since 1948. Who is this record credited to?
    a) Don Bradman
    b) Ricky Ponting
    c) Alastair Cook

11. According to the inscription on the Ashes Urn, who 'goes back with the urn'?
    a) Hornby
    b) Ivo
    c) Donald

12. Since 2005, which medal is given to the 'Man of the Series' in the Ashes?
    a) Richie Benaud and Jim Laker
    b) Compton-Miller
    c) Benson and Hedges

13. After Syd Gregory, who has played the most number of matches in the Ashes?
    a) Colin Cowdrey
    b) Steve Waugh
    c) Warwick Armstrong

14. In 1998, Lord Darnley's daughter-in-law claimed that the original Ashes Urn contained...
    a) Burnt bails
    b) Mud from Lord's cricket ground
    c) Remains of her mother-in-law's veil

15. Who has umpired the most number of Tests in the Ashes?
    a) Steve Bucknor
    b) R.M. Crockett
    c) Rudi Koertzen

16. In the 1882 series, what did both sides agree on for the first and last time ever?

   a)   To use a new ball at both ends
   b)   To play each innings on a separate pitch
   c)   To play a day and night match

17.   Who said, 'I don't want to see you, Mr Warner.
      There are two teams out there. One is trying to play
      cricket and the other is not'?
      a)   Donald Bradman
      b)   Bill Woodfull
      c)   Bert Oldfield

18.   When the Ashes are held in England, at which
      ground is the last Test traditionally played?
      a)   Old Trafford
      b)   Kennington Oval
      c)   Trent Bridge

19.   What is the name of the urn-shaped trophy
      presented to the winner of the Ashes?
      a)   The MCC Waterford Crystal trophy
      b)   The MCC Triple Crown Trophy
      c)   The MCC Vince Lombardi Trophy

20.   Who is the only man to play in the Ashes for both
      England and Australia?
      a)   Billy Midwinter
      b)   Alfred Shaw
      c)   Jack Blackham

SPORTY FACTS

▸ J.M. Barrie, the author of *Peter Pan*, was an ardent cricket fan. In the late 1800s, he created an amateur cricket team called *The Allahakbarries* and got some of the most famous writers of the time, including Arthur Conan Doyle, P.G. Wodehouse, A.A. Milne and Jerome K. Jerome, to play on the team.

▸ Virat Kohli has a fruity nickname—Chikoo. The origin of the name is very interesting. The Delhi team, of which he was a member, was playing a Ranji Trophy match in Mumbai. At the time, he had not even played a total of 10 first-class matches. One evening, he went out and got a haircut. After he returned, he asked his colleagues to comment on his new look. 'Not bad, you look like a Chikoo (Sapodilla),' remarked Ajit Chowdhary, the assistant coach. The name stuck.

▸ Viswanathan Anand learned to play chess from his mother when he was only six years old. He became the youngest Indian to earn an international master title by the time he was 15.

▸ Tug of War was an official event in five modern Olympic Games—from Paris 1900 to Antwerp 1920 (excluding the 1916 Games). According to the rules, the team that pulled the other team six feet over a line within five minutes was declared winner. If there was no clear winner, then the team that pulled its rival team the furthest, won.

▶ Lateral epicondylitis is a painful condition that affects the area around the elbow, and is generally caused by repeated twisting of the wrist and the arm. Though it is popularly called tennis elbow, few people actually get it by playing tennis.

ATHLETICS

1. In 1984, he equalled Jesse Owens's performance by winning 4 golds in a single Olympics. He is also the only man to have won the long jump Olympic title four consecutive times. Name him.
    a) Edwin Moses
    b) Carl Lewis
    c) Daley Thompson

2. Milkha Singh, who won India's first Commonwealth gold, was nicknamed 'The Flying Sikh' by...
    a) Mahatma Gandhi
    b) General Ayub Khan
    c) Jawaharlal Nehru

3. Which scientist, a member of the Walton Athletic Club, came 5th in the AAA Marathon in 1947?
    a) Carl Sagan
    b) Edwin Hubble
    c) Alan Turing

4. At the 1960 Summer Olympics, although Wilma Rudolph ran the finals in the 100-metre dash in 11.0 seconds, it was not credited as a world record. Why?
    a) Because it was wind-assisted
    b) Because she failed the dope test
    c) Because she wasn't wearing standard footwear

5. According to Usain Bolt, his 'To Di World' victory pose was inspired by...
    a) A Jamaican folk dance
    b) An advertisement
    c) An archer's stance

6. Whose 21-year-old record was broken by Olympic champion Renaud Lavillenie?
    a) Michael Johnson
    b) Sergey Bubka
    c) Carl Lewis

7. *Golden Girl* is the autobiography of...
    a) Anju Bobby George
    b) M.D. Valsamma
    c) P.T. Usha

8. The 'shot' in shot put is a...
    a) Hammer
    b) Metal Ball
    c) Scabbard

9. At the 2012 London Olympics, the team that won gold in the 4×100 m relay race, in a record 36.84 seconds, comprised Nesta Carter, Michael Frater, Yohan Blake and...
    a) Usain Bolt
    b) Michael Johnson
    c) Kenenisa Bekele

10. According to legend, the concept of which sport can be traced back to the Tailteann Games in Tara,

Ireland, where the Celtic warrior Culchulainn gripped a chariot wheel by its axle, whirled it around and threw it far away?
a) Hammer throw
b) Shot put
c) Discus throw

11. Popularised by the Olympic champion Dick Fosbury, the Fosbury Flop is a technique used in which athletics event?
a) Pole vault
b) Long jump
c) High jump

12. Although Yelena Isinbayeva managed to qualify for the 2016 Olympic Games, she was unable to participate because...
a) The Russian athletics team was banned after the discovery of state-sponsored doping programme.
b) She defected to the US.
c) She was expecting her first child.

13. Which is the longest athletics event on the Olympic programme and the only athletics event at major championships still contested by only men?
a) 3000 m steeplechase
b) Marathon
c) 50 km race walk

14. Which of these was once known as hop, step and jump?

   a)   Pole vault
   b)   Long jump
   c)   Triple jump

15. The first event contested in the ancient Olympic
     Games, a sprint of about 192 metres, was called...
     a)   Relay race
     b)   Stadium race
     c)   Steeplechase

16. Much to the delight of his Greek countrymen,
     Spyridon Louis won which event at the modern
     Olympic Games in 1896?
     a)   Javelin throw
     b)   Marathon
     c)   Archery

17. In 1989, which athlete designed the uniforms for the
     NBA team, Indiana Pacers?
     a)   Florence Griffith Joyner
     b)   Marion Jones
     c)   Jackie Joyner-Kersee

18. In 2016, who won the silver medal in the women's
     shotput F53 event and became India's first woman to
     win a medal at the Paralympics?
     a)   Pooja Khanna
     b)   Deepa Malik
     c)   Karamjyoti Dalal

19. Who is the first Indian athlete to win a track gold at
     any World Championship event (including juniors)?

a) Annu Rani
b) Hima Das
c) Anju Bobby George

20. 'I always loved running—it was something you could do by yourself and under your own power. You could go in any direction...on the strength of your feet and the courage of your lungs.' Who said this?
a) Jesse Owens
b) Paavo Nurmi
c) Wilma Rudolph

SPORTY FACTS

▸ The 2010 film *Secretariat* is based on the life of a legendary thoroughbred racehorse from the USA.

▸ The first woman to be listed as a winner at the Ancient Olympic Games was Kyniska, daughter of the King of Sparta. The victory wreath, in equestrian events of the time, was awarded to the owner and not the rider of the horse. She received it for owning the horse that won the four-horse chariot race at the 96th Olympiads.

▸ In 1999, Leander Paes and Mahesh Bhupathi reached the doubles finals of all four Grand Slam tournaments, winning the French Open and Wimbledon but losing in the Australian and U.S. Opens.

▸ The two most commonly recognized stances in boxing are called orthodox and southpaw. An orthodox boxing stance is one where the left hand and the left foot are forward. In the southpaw stance, the right hand and the right foot are forward.

▸ The loincloth worn by sumo wrestlers is called a *mawashi*. It is made of different types of materials such as silk and canvas.

BADMINTON

1. A version of badminton was played by British army officers stationed in India. By what name was it known then?
    a) Goa
    b) Patna
    c) Poona

2. Who became the first non-Asian woman to win the Olympic badminton singles gold?
    a) Tine Baun
    b) Carolina Marin
    c) Christinna Pedersen

3. The song 'Dhal Gaya Din', centred on a game of badminton, from the film *Humjoli* is picturised on...
    a) Sulakshana Pandit-Dharmendra
    b) Leena Chandavarkar-Jeetendra
    c) Aruna Irani-Rishi Kapoor

4. In 1991, the Uttar Pradesh Badminton Association inaugurated a tournament in memory of the 1982 Commonwealth Games men's singles champion. Who was he?
    a) Prakash Padukone
    b) Syed Modi
    c) Dipankar Bhattacharjee

5. Who was the first Indian to achieve the number one world ranking in badminton?
    a) Saina Nehwal
    b) Prakash Padukone
    c) Pulela Gopichand

6. Historically, the shuttlecock was a small cork hemisphere with 16 feathers of which bird?
    a) Owl
    b) Hen
    c) Goose

7. The body is shaped like a shuttlecock. The lid is a replica of the Borobudur Temple in Indonesia. Name the trophy.
    a) Herbert Scheele Trophy
    b) Thomas Cup
    c) Sudirman Cup

8. At 29 all, how many points does one have to score to win that game?
    a) One
    b) Two
    c) Three

9. Apart from red and yellow, which colour card is used in badminton?
    a) Black
    b) Green
    c) Orange

10. Which trophy is presented for outstanding and

exceptional services to badminton?
a) Suhandinata Cup
b) Herbert Scheele Trophy
c) Uber Cup

11. In 1899, which tournament was first held at the London Scottish Regiment Drill Hall?
a) Uber Cup
b) All England Open
c) The White Nights

12. From 1992 to 2008, players from which continent won 69 of the 76 medals available in Olympic competition?
a) Europe
b) Asia
c) Africa

13. The game badminton is named after…
a) An ancient game
b) The country estate of the dukes of Beaufort
c) A footwear company

14. In badminton, who won the first-ever 'Super Grand Slam' by winning all nine of its premier titles?
a) Viktor Axelsen
b) Peter Gade
c) Lin Dan

15. Who became the first Indian badminton player to win a silver medal at the Olympics?
a) Saina Nehwal

b) P.V. Sindhu
c) Jwala Gutta

16. A shot hit softly and with finesse to fall rapidly and close to the net on the opponent's side, is called a...
   a) Clear
   b) Smash
   c) Drop shot

17. Badminton debuted as a full-medal Olympic sport in...
   a) Barcelona (1992)
   b) Seoul (1988)
   c) Atlanta (1996)

18. Unless otherwise arranged, a match consists of the best of...
   a) 2 games of 15 points
   b) 3 games of 21 points
   c) 4 games of 25 points

19. When the base of a shuttle hits the frame of a racquet, it results in a...
   a) Raquet shot
   b) Frame shot
   c) Wood shot

20. What is the title of Saina Nehwal's autobiography?
   a) *Unbreakable*
   b) *Playing It My Way*
   c) *Playing to Win, My Life On and Off Court*

SPORTY FACTS

▸ Roger Bannister, the first athlete to run the mile in less than four minutes, gave up competitive running at the height of his career because he wanted to concentrate on studying medicine. He said, 'I shall have to give up international athletics. I shall not have sufficient time to put up a first-class performance. There would be little satisfaction for me in a second-rate performance, and it would be wrong to give one when representing my country.'

▸ The hippodrome was an ancient Greek stadium designed for horse racing and chariot racing.

▸ The Olympic gold medal is not made of solid gold. The 1912 Games were the last to award gold medals made of solid gold. Today, each medal is made of 93 per cent silver, six per cent copper and just one per cent gold.

▸ In 2018, the WTA dedicated its World No.1 trophy to Chris Evert by officially naming it the 'Chris Evert WTA World No.1 Trophy'. Simona Halep became the first recipient of the trophy.

▸ In 2006, a *shaman* from Ecuador visited all 12 World Cup venues in Germany to banish evil spirits before the tournament began. Incidentally, the team reached the Round of 16 before being eliminated—their best performance till date.

BOARD GAMES

1. Which game was initially rejected by Parker Brothers for '52 fundamental playing errors'?
    a) Scrabble
    b) Monopoly
    c) Chess

2. Which game, invented by a New Yorker named Alfred Butts, was formerly called 'Criss-Cross Words'?
    a) Scrabble
    b) The Game of Life
    c) Pictionary

3. What originated as educational devices to teach geography in eighteenth-century England?
    a) Jigsaw puzzles
    b) Trivial Pursuit
    c) Diplomacy

4. Which Mughal emperor is said to have played chess with live models at the Pachisi Court in Fatehpur Sikri?
    a) Humayun
    b) Akbar
    c) Shah Jahan

5. The Satyajit Ray-directed film *Shatranj Ke Khilari*, was based on a short story by which famous author?
    a) Munshi Premchand
    b) Rabindranath Tagore
    c) R.K. Narayan

6. In which board game would you meet characters named Colonel Mustard, Miss Scarlet and Mrs Peacock?
    a) Pandemic
    b) Pictionary
    c) Cluedo

7. Which game, created by the thirteenth-century poet saint Gyandev, was originally called Mokshapat?
    a) Snakes and Ladders
    b) Chess
    c) Ludo

8. The object of which game is to conquer the world by occupying every territory on the board, thus eliminating all your opponents?
    a) Risk
    b) Ludo
    c) Ticket to Ride

9. Which board game was developed by Chris Haney, a picture editor at the *Montreal Gazette* and Scott Abbott, a sports journalist for *The Canadian Press*?
    a) Trivial Pursuit
    b) Monopoly
    c) Scrabble

10. In which of these games do players themselves serve as the key board game pieces?
   a) Twister
   b) Blokus
   c) Connect 4

11. The name of which game comes from the Latin words for 'I play'?
   a) Ludo
   b) Mancala
   c) Shogi

12. What is played on a star-shaped board consisting of a 61-hole central hexagon and six 10-hole equilateral triangles that extend outward from each side?
   a) Chinese Checkers
   b) Risk
   c) Guess Who?

13. Played by the ancient Romans, Ludus Duodecim Scriptorum, which translates to 'Twelve-lined Game', was very similar to...
   a) Backgammon
   b) Checkers
   c) Battleship

14. Which game was designed by Rob Angel, a waiter, who randomly picked a word, drew it, and made party-goers guess the word?
   a) Pictionary
   b) Cranium
   c) Clay Mania

15. Invented by Goro Hasegawa, which of these is used by medical institutions for rehabilitation of patients with encephalopathia, a disease that affects brain function?
    a) Othello
    b) Axis and Allies
    c) Scrabble

16. Shogi is a Japanese form of chess. How many squares does the shogi chessboard have?
    a) 49
    b) 64
    c) 81

17. Which of these games is also called The Mill?
    a) Nine Men's Morris
    b) Game of the Goose
    c) Stratego

18. Nyout-nol-ki is an ancient cross-and-circle board game of...
    a) Korean origin
    b) Chinese origin
    c) German origin

19. In Scrabble, the highest number of points that can be scored on the first go is 128 with the word...
    a) muzjiks
    b) caziques
    c) euouae

20. In which board game do you need to trace Mister X's route all around London?
    a) Capital Punishment
    b) Scotland Yard
    c) Twister

SPORTY FACTS

▸ Swapna Burman, the first Indian athlete to win a gold medal in heptathlon at the Asian Games, has six toes on each foot.

▸ In 1924, Edith Cummings, a golf champion, became the first woman athlete to appear on the cover of *Time* magazine.

▸ Cricketer Ricky Ponting was nicknamed Punter because he used to bet on horses when he was in his teens.

▸ The Akshay Kumar-starrer *Gold* was the first Bollywood film to release in Saudi Arabia. The film, directed by Reema Kagti, was inspired by the Indian hockey team's iconic win at the 1948 London Olympics.

▸ Vasbert Drakes, a West Indian fast bowler, is one of the few players in first-class cricket to have been timed-out. He met this fate at a Border vs Free State match in East London in 2002. At the time of being declared 'timed-out', he was not just away from the ground but also from the country—his flight from Colombo was severely delayed.

BOXING AND WRESTLING

1. Mr Khardekar, the Principal of Rajaram College in Kolhapur, mortgaged his house for Rs 7,000 to sponsor whose trip to the Olympics?
   a) Yogeshwar Dutt
   b) Maruti Mane
   c) K.D. Jadhav

2. Who was the first heavyweight boxer to simultaneously hold the WBA, WBC and IBF titles?
   a) Mike Tyson
   b) George Foreman
   c) Jack Dempsey

3. What is the ring in which sumo wrestling bouts are held called?
   a) Tatami
   b) Dojo
   c) Dohyo

4. Which American president's wrestling exploits earned him the 'Outstanding American' honour in the National Wrestling Hall of Fame?
   a) Abraham Lincoln
   b) Benjamin Franklin
   c) George Washington

5. Who was the first Indian female wrestler to win an
    Olympic medal?
    a) Sakshi Malik
    b) Geeta Phogat
    c) Kavita Devi

6. Whose routine of punching sides of meat stored
    in a refrigerated room in a slaughterhouse in
    Philadelphia inspired the famous scene in the
    Sylvester Stallone starrer *Rocky*?
    a) Muhammad Ali
    b) Joe Frazier
    c) Floyd Mayweather Jr.

7. In 2012, the road connecting Churachandpur town
    to the office of the deputy commissioner in Manipur
    was named after which sportsperson?
    a) M.C. Mary Kom
    b) Mirabai Chanu
    c) Shiva Thapa

8. Among these, which boxing division is the heaviest?
    a) Flyweight
    b) Minimumweight
    c) Featherweight

9. The 1996 film *When We Were Kings* revolves around
    which match?
    a) The Rumble in the Jungle
    b) Thrilla in Manila
    c) The Fight of the Century

10. A part of whose ear did Mike Tyson bite off during a fight at the heavyweight championship?
    a) Riddick Bowe
    b) James Douglas
    c) Evander Holyfield

11. Jean Exbrayat, who is credited with setting the rule of not allowing holds below the waist, the most easily recognized characteristic of modern Greco-Roman wrestling, was a soldier in whose army?
    a) Alexander the Great
    b) Napoleon Bonaparte
    c) Joseph Stalin

12. Among wrestlers, who was the first to win the Rajiv Gandhi Khel Ratna award?
    a) Yogeshwar Dutt
    b) Dara Singh
    c) Sushil Kumar

13. A takedown in which a wrestler is brought across the opponent's shoulders is known as...
    a) Fireman's carry
    b) Gut wrench
    c) Half nelson

14. Name the ninth Marquess of Queensberry under whose sponsorship the Marquess of Queensberry rules were first published in 1867.
    a) Francis Archibald Kelhead Douglas
    b) John Sholto Douglas
    c) Archibald William Douglas

15. In a boxing ring, if the boxers' corners are called red and blue, what are the other two corners called?
    a) White
    b) Black
    c) Pink

16. What is another name for boxing?
    a) Pugilism
    b) Phlegmy
    c) Perique

17. Which Indian boxer made his Bollywood debut in the film *Fugly* in 2014?
    a) Vijender Singh
    b) Akhil Kumar
    c) Jitender Kumar

18. In 1978, who won the World Heavyweight title just one year and one month after turning professional?
    a) Leon Spinks
    b) Mike Tyson
    c) Joe Louis

19. Greco-Roman wrestling originated in which country in imitation of classical Greek and Roman representations of the sport?
    a) Spain
    b) Bulgaria
    c) France

20. Fill in the blank to complete this quote by Muhammad Ali, 'The man who has no _____

has no wings.'
a) Intelligence
b) Imagination
c) Passion

SPORTY FACTS

▸ In 1971, Billie Jean King became the first female athlete to earn over US $100,000 in prize money.

▸ In 1969, El Salvador, a country in Central America, declared war on its neighbour Honduras after it was defeated in a football match. The war has been variously described as 'Football War', 'Soccer War' and '100-Hour-War'.

▸ In 2014, Cristiano Ronaldo became the first player to score a goal in every minute of a football match.

▸ The first modern trampoline, a bed-like structure made of stretchable material for tumbling, was built by George Nissen and Larry Griswold, in Iowa, in 1934. Though it was initially used by tumblers, astronauts and others who wanted to improve their acrobatic skills for sports like diving and gymnastics, it became a full-fledged sport in itself later. It made its first appearance at the 2000 Games in Sydney.

▸ The mascot of the 2020 Tokyo Games is called Miraitowa. The name comes from two Japanese words meaning future and eternity. The mascot was selected by the children of Japanese primary schools.

CARD GAMES

1. In a standard deck of playing cards, which king appears to have a sword driven into his head, earning him the nickname 'Suicide King'?
    a) King of Diamonds
    b) King of Spades
    c) King of Hearts

2. In bridge, what is a yarborough?
    a) A hand with no card above a nine
    b) Another name for the rank 2 cards
    c) A card laid on the table face-up

3. Which game, previously known as demon, was named after a Saratoga saloon owner who sold players a deck of cards for $50 and paid them $5 for each card they managed to play off in the game?
    a) Canfield
    b) Hanafuda
    c) Cuarenta

4. In the Japanese card game hanafuda, the deck of 48 cards is divided into 12 suits of four cards. What is each suit named after?
    a) A month of the year
    b) A western zodiac sign
    c) A Japanese deity

5. Ruff and honours was one of the names of which card game?
   a) Whist
   b) Crazy Eights
   c) Speed

6. In Italian playing cards, what are hearts, diamonds and spades replaced by?
   a) Coins, cups and swords
   b) Stone, paper and scissors
   c) Flower, star and fish

7. Who played the role of Prof. Venkat Subramaniam in the film *Teen Patti*?
   a) Amitabh Bachchan
   b) Vinod Khanna
   c) Rishi Kapoor

8. Skat is the national card game of which country?
   a) Germany
   b) USA
   c) Italy

9. What made its first appearance in a deck of playing cards in 1857?
   a) The Joker
   b) The Queen of Hearts
   c) The Jack of Diamonds

10. In a deck of playing cards, which card is called the 'Curse of Scotland'?
    a) Nine of Diamonds

b) Ace of Spades
c) Jack of Clubs

11. Which of these was invented by E.T. Baker in a New York club in 1909?
a) Gin rummy
b) Canasta
c) Bezique

12. Harold Stirling Vanderbilt, on a cruise from San Francisco to Havana, perfected the rules of...
a) Contract bridge
b) Crazy Eights
c) Spit

13. In 1935, card manufacturers tried to introduce a fifth suit. What did they call it in the US?
a) Eagles
b) Crowns
c) Saucers

14. In which book did the Queen of Hearts say, 'Off with their heads!'?
a) *Alice's Adventures in Wonderland*
b) *Gulliver's Travels*
c) *Animal Farm*

15. In 1793, French authorities banned the depictions of royalty on playing cards. Kings, queens and jacks became...
a) Liberties, equalities and fraternities
b) Blood, toil and tears
c) Faster, higher and stronger

16. According to International Playing Card Society, in 1765, England began to stamp a single card to indicate that tax had been paid for the deck of cards. Which card was it?
    a) Ace of Spades
    b) Jack of Diamonds
    c) Queen of Hearts

17. Which of these is another name for blackjack?
    a) 21
    b) 25
    c) 27

18. Which Russian author wrote a short story titled 'The Queen of Spades'?
    a) Alexander Pushkin
    b) Anton Chekov
    c) Vladimir Nabokov

19. In which book would you come across the line: 'He calls the knaves, Jacks, this boy!'?
    a) *The House of Mirth*
    b) *Great Expectations*
    c) *Mansfield Park*

20. Which was the only film for which Robert Redford was ever nominated for an Academy Award as Best Actor?
    a) *The Sting*
    b) *Spy Game*
    c) *The Gambler*

SPORTY FACTS

▸ The famous yellow cover of Wisden Cricketers' Almanack first appeared on the 75th edition in 1938.

▸ In the *Boy Meets Curl* episode of *The Simpsons*, the characters Homer and Marge were selected to represent the United States in mixed-doubles curling at the 2010 Calgary Olympics.

▸ The word 'arena' refers to an area of level land surrounded by seating, used for sports and other public events. It comes from the Latin harena or arena, meaning sand or sand-strewn place of combat.

▸ Smriti Mandhana became the first Indian female cricketer to score a double century in a one-day match, using Rahul Dravid's practice bat.

▸ Alexis Olympia, daughter of Serena Williams and Alexis Ohanian, became the youngest girl on the cover of *Vogue* US when she appeared with her mother on the cover of the February 2018 edition of the magazine. She was just three months old at the time of the shoot.

ENTERTAINMENT AND SPORTS

1. Which sportsperson made his debut with the 2013 film *Rajdhani Express*?
   a) Leander Paes
   b) Ajay Jadeja
   c) Salil Ankola

2. Who took just one rupee as a token from Rakeysh Omprakash Mehra to allow the director to make a film on his life?
   a) M.S. Dhoni
   b) Milkha Singh
   c) Azharuddin

3. In China, which film was released as *Shuai Jiao Baba*, which translates as '*Let's Wrestle, Dad*'?
   a) *Sultan*
   b) *Dangal*
   c) *Gold*

4. In 1982, Vangelis won the Academy Award for Music (Original Score) for which film?
   a) *Chariots of Fire*
   b) *Bull Durham*
   c) *The Natural*

5. The 1981 TV film *Miracle on Ice* revolved around which sport?

    a)   Ice Hockey
    b)   Figure skating
    c)   Curling

6.   How do we better know Begum Ayesha Sultana, who married a cricketer on 27 December 1969?
    a)   Sharmila Tagore
    b)   Sangeeta Bijlani
    c)   Reena Roy

7.   This sportsperson starred in a Marathi film titled *Savli Premachi*. He also made a cameo in the 1988 film *Maalamaal*. Name him.
    a)   Sunil Gavaskar
    b)   Lala Amarnath
    c)   Syed Kirmani

8.   Which film shows how Billy Beane, the boss of Oakland Athletics, assembled a baseball team by employing computer-generated analysis to acquire new players?
    a)   *Seabiscuit*
    b)   *Moneyball*
    c)   *The Blind Side*

9.   The 2010 film *Invictus* revolves around which sport?
    a)   Baseball
    b)   Ice hockey
    c)   Rugby

10.   Who was the director of the 2002 film *Bend It Like Beckham*?

a) Gurinder Chadha
b) James Cameron
c) Deepa Mehta

11. The film *Unbroken* revolves around Olympian Louis Zamperini's harrowing 47-day journey in a raft after a plane crash. Who was the director of the film?
   a) Angelina Jolie
   b) Jodie Foster
   c) Ethan Hawke

12. The statue of which fictional sportsperson is located at the bottom of the stairs at the Philadelphia Museum of Art?
   a) Billy Hope
   b) Rocky Balboa
   c) Margaret Fitzgerald

13. From which famous 1980 film is the quote, 'You never got me down, Ray!'?
   a) *Raging Bull*
   b) *The Fighter*
   c) *Jerry Maguire*

14. Which film is based on the book titled *Rope Burns* by F.X. Toole?
   a) *Million Dollar Baby*
   b) *The Wrestler*
   c) *The Fighter*

15. Which Oliver Stone-directed film is famous for Al Pacino's pregame speech 'Life is just a game of inches'?
    a) *Any Given Sunday*
    b) *Blue Chips*
    c) *He Got Game*

16. Which 1981 film starred professional footballers Bobby Moore, Osvaldo Ardiles, Kazimierz Deyna, Paul Van Himst, Mike Summerbee, Hallvar Thoresen, Werner Roth and Pelī?
    a) *Escape to Victory*
    b) *Miracle*
    c) *Goon*

17. Which film was shot in Jam Kunaria village near Bhuj in Gujarat's Kutch district in 2001?
    a) *Lagaan*
    b) *Jo Jeeta Wohi Sikandar*
    c) *Dangal*

18. Who developed his own technique—jeet kune do—a blend of ancient kung fu, fencing, boxing and philosophy?
    a) Jackie Chan
    b) Bruce Lee
    c) Jet Li

19. Which 2007 film follows two rival figure skaters, Will Ferrell and Jon Heder, who must team up if they want to continue their skating careers?
    a) *Blades of Glory*

b) *Miracle on Ice*
c) *Friday Night Lights*

20. The song 'Black Superman' by Johnny Wakelin & the Kinshasa Band was about...
a) Jesse Owens
b) Muhammad Ali
c) Arthur Ashe

SPORTY FACTS

▸ Water polo was originally called 'football-in-the-water' in Great Britain, the country of its origin. Though it resembles football and basketball more than polo, it gets its name water polo from the earlier avatar of the sport in which participants sat on barrels painted like horses and hit the ball with sticks.

▸ Viswanathan Anand, Roger Federer, Donald Bradman, Paavo Nurmi, all have celestial bodies named after them.

▸ The word checkmate comes from Persian words 'shah' and 'mat' meaning 'the king is dead'.

▸ The Wanderers Stadium in Johannesburg, South Africa, is also known as the 'Bullring' because of its intimidating atmosphere for visiting teams.

▸ In the *Harry Potter* universe, the sport quidditch is named after Queerditch Marsh, the place where the first modern game of quidditch was played.

FORMULA 1

1. What structural mandatory addition was made to all 2018 Formula 1 cars to protect the driver's head from flying debris?
    a) The diffuser
    b) The halo
    c) The endplates

2. If you were a Formula 1 driver and you saw a race marshal waving a yellow flag, it would mean...
    a) There is danger ahead and you need to slow down
    b) The session has been stopped
    c) You have been excluded from the race

3. Starring Chris Hemsworth and Daniel Brühl, the 2013 film *Rush* depicted the rivalry between Formula 1 drivers James Hunt and...
    a) Alain Prost
    b) Ayrton Senna
    c) Niki Lauda

4. Since 1994, all Williams F1 cars have carried a logo dedicated to which F1 legend?
    a) Nelson Piquet
    b) Nigel Mansell
    c) Ayrton Senna

5. With which team did Michael Schumacher begin his Formula 1 career in 1991?
   a) Ferrari
   b) Jordan
   c) Benetton

6. What is the name of the circuit that was host to the Indian Grand Prix between 2011 and 2013?
   a) Buddh International Circuit
   b) Ashoka International Circuit
   c) Mahavira International Circuit

7. The first F1 world championship race was won by Giuseppe Farina in a...
   a) Maserati
   b) Ferrari
   c) Alfa Romeo

8. Who is the only driver to not qualify, not finish and be disqualified all in the same Formula One race?
   a) Klaus Ludwig
   b) Hans Heyer
   c) Bob Wollek

9. With 91 race victories to his name, who holds the record of winning the most number of races in F1?
   a) Alain Prost
   b) Michael Schumacher
   c) Lewis Hamilton

10. Which of these father and son duos has not clinched world championship crowns?

    a)   Graham and Damon Hill
    b)   Gilles and Jacques Villeneuve
    c)   Keke and Nico Rosberg

11.   In 1948, the Royal Automobile Club held the first Grand Prix at this former wartime airfield. How do we know this circuit today?
    a)   Monaco
    b)   Silverstone
    c)   Hockenheimring

12.   When he won the Spanish Grand Prix in 2016 at the age of 18 years and 228 days, he became the youngest race winner in F1 history. Name him.
    a)   Sebastian Vettel
    b)   Max Verstappen
    c)   Lewis Hamilton

13.   Who is the first female driver to score championship points in Fomula 1?
    a)   Giovanna Amati
    b)   Lella Lombardi
    c)   Maria Teresa de Filippis

14.   What is the strictly controlled overtaking aid used by drivers that alters the angle of the rear wing flap to reduce drag called?
    a)   KERS
    b)   DRS
    c)   ABS

15.   The racing strategy in which a car trailing behind

another pits early, returns to clear track and then puts in faster laps to ensure it emerges ahead once the other car has made its pit stop, is called...
a) Hopscotching
b) Slingshooting
c) Undercutting

16. During the first phase of qualifying, any driver who fails to set a lap within 107 per cent of the fastest Q1 time, will...
a) Not be allowed to start the race
b) Get a 10 second penalty in the pits
c) Have 5 championship points deducted

17. What do you call a tight sequence of corners in alternate directions, usually inserted into a circuit to slow the cars, often just before what had been a high-speed corner?
a) Camber
b) Bargeboard
c) Chicane

18. The place where the team owner, managers and engineers spend the race, usually under an awning to keep sun and rain off their monitors is called...
a) The Pit Wall
b) The Plank
c) Pole position

19. In 2007, who beat Fernando Alonso and Lewis Hamilton by a single point to win the driver's championship?

a) Rubens Barrichello
b) Mark Webber
c) Kimi Raikkonen

20. This team made its debut in 2009 when Honda was purchased after its withdrawal from F1 the pervious year. It also went on to win the Contructor's Championship the same year. Name the team.
a) Red Bull Racing
b) Brawn GP
c) Marussia F1 Team

SPORTY FACTS

▶ In 2009, Usain Bolt adopted a three-month-old cheetah cub and named him Lightning Bolt.

▶ Wimbledon, one of the four Grand Slam tennis tournaments, is the only Grand Slam still played on the game's original surface—grass. It was first held in 1877.

▶ In 1998, all the members of a football team were struck dead on the football field by a freak bolt of lightning in the Democratic Republic of Congo. Strangely, the opponent team remained unhurt!

▶ Milkha Singh was the first Indian to win a gold medal in athletics at the Commonwealth Games. He won gold in the 440 yards sprint at the 1958 Games in Cardiff, with a timing of 46.6 s.

▶ In 2018, Tham Luang Nang Non cave in northern Thailand rose to prominence as a tourist spot after a team of experts from across the world came together and saved 12 members of a junior soccer team and their coach who were trapped in the underground network for 18 days.

FIFA WORLD CUP

1. In the Maradonian Church, founded by Alejandro
    Verón, Hīctor Campomar and Hernán Amez, the
    members celebrate Easter on 22 June in honour
    of...
    a) Maradona's birth
    b) The match between Argentina and England in
        the 1986 FIFA World Cup in which Maradona
        led his side to victory.
    c) Maradona's first FIFA World Cup goal

2. Which country won the inaugural FIFA World Cup
    in 1930?
    a) Brazil
    b) Argentina
    c) Uruguay

3. Which country was the first one to be allowed to
    keep the World Cup permanently?
    a) Argentina
    b) France
    c) Brazil

4. 'Only three people have ever silenced 200,000 people
    at the Maracana with a single gesture: Frank Sinatra,
    Pope John Paul II, and I.' Who said this for having
    scored the winning goal at the 1950 World Cup final?
    a) Obdulio Varela

    b) Alcides Ghiggia
    c) Víctor Rodríguez Andrade

5. Which was the first team to successfully defend the FIFA World Cup title?
    a) Germany
    b) France
    c) Italy

6. In 2018, at the age of 45 years and 161 days, who became the oldest player to play in a World Cup?
    a) Essam El Hadary
    b) Gianluigi Buffon
    c) Robin van Persie

7. Laurent Blanc was the first player in the history of the FIFA World Cup to…
    a) Score a golden goal
    b) Receive a red card
    c) Be substituted

8. According to legend, which requirement in the 1950 World Cup forced India to withdraw from the competition?
    a) Playing with shoes
    b) Playing in team uniform
    c) Using protective gear

9. Though the Russian national football team ranked 70th according to FIFA official rankings, prior to the World Cup 2018, they qualified for it because…
    a) They had won gold in Olympics 2016

b) One place is reserved for the host nation

c) They were a wild card entry

10. In 1978, which country became the first African team to win a match in the FIFA World Cup?
    a) Ghana
    b) Cameroon
    c) Tunisia

11. In 1999, who was named Coach of the Century by FIFA?
    a) Louis van Gaal
    b) Albert Batteux
    c) Rinus Michels

12. Apart from Panama, which other country qualified for the World Cup finals for the first time in 2018?
    a) Kazakhstan
    b) Egypt
    c) Iceland

13. All the champions of the Cup have been from Europe or...
    a) Africa
    b) South America
    c) Asia

14. The 1970 World Cup saw the introduction of red and yellow cards, and also a provision for substitution. In which country was it held?
    a) Russia

b) Mexico

c) Uruguay

15. Who is the only player to have won three FIFA World Cup winners' medals?
a) Diego Maradona
b) Pelī
c) Zinedine Zidane

16. Which is the only team to qualify for every edition of the tournament?
a) Germany
b) Brazil
c) England

17. Total Football, a tactical theory in football in which any outfield player, except the goalkeeper, can take over the role of any other player in a team, was made famous by the Netherlands team in the...
a) 1974 FIFA World Cup
b) 1978 FIFA World Cup
c) 1986 FIFA World Cup

18. Which was the first World Cup finals to be televised in colour to a global audience?
a) 1958
b) 1970
c) 1974

19. Who is the only player to have scored twice on his birthday in the World Cup—against Kuwait in 1982 and against Brazil in 1986?

    a)   Michel Platini
    b)   Paolo Maldini
    c)   Bobby Charlton

20. Who scored a record 13 goals in the only FIFA World Cup tournament he ever played?
    a)   Just Fontaine
    b)   Paul Breitner
    c)   Carlos Alberto

SPORTY FACTS

▸ The 2018 Winter Olympics was hosted in PyeongChang, South Korea. The height of the Olympic torch was exactly 700 mm, representing the altitude of PyeongChang, which is 700 metres above sea level.

▸ During the Egyptian presidential election in 2018, more than one million people struck out the names of the two candidates, President Abdel Fattah al-Sisi and his opponent, Moussa Mostafa Moussa, and replaced them with that of their country's national hero, footballer Mohamed Salah.

▸ Though the origin of the term Mexican wave is disputed, it is said to have its roots in the 1986 FIFA World Cup in Mexico, where it was widely seen for the first time.

▸ In 1976, Princess Anne, daughter of Queen Elizabeth II and Prince Philip, became the first member of the British Royal Family to compete in the Olympic Games. She rode the Queen's horse, Goodwill, in the equestrian three-day event that year.

▸ A statue of Zinedine Zidane's infamous headbutt on Marco Materazzi, during the final of the 2006 FIFA World Cup, was unveiled at the Centre Pompidou in Paris in 2012. The five-feet-tall bronze statue was sculpted by Algerian artist Adel Abdessemed.

FOOTBALL

1. Which footballer was described as 'Pythagoras in boots' for the complexity and precision of his angled passes?
   a) Johan Cruyff
   b) Sergio Batista
   c) Cafu

2. 'He's the best rival I ever had. I guess that's enough to define him,' Diego Maradona wrote in his autobiography about his adversary in two World Cups. Who was he talking about?
   a) Gerd Muller
   b) Lothar Herbert Matthaeus
   c) Pele

3. In March 2016, who became the fastest player in Europe to score 350 goals for a single club?
   a) Lionel Messi
   b) Cristiano Ronaldo
   c) Neymar Jr.

4. Who became the first non-European player to win the PFA Players of the Year award?
   a) Sergio Aguero
   b) Neymar
   c) Luis Suarez

5. Which footballer's original name is Manuel Francisco dos Santos?
   a) Josimar
   b) Garrincha
   c) Didi

6. In 1886, workers from Woolwich Armaments Factory decided to form a football team. They called themselves Dial Square as a reference to the sundial atop the entrance to the factory. What is the club presently known as?
   a) Chelsea
   b) Tottenham Hotspur
   c) Arsenal

7. Who is the longest-serving manager during the English Premier League era?
   a) Arsene Wenger
   b) Sam Allardyce
   c) Josī Mourinho

8. The 'Tiki-Taka' style of playing football is associated with which country?
   a) Germany
   b) England
   c) Spain

9. Which European trophy becomes the property of any club that wins the competition five times or three years in a row?
   a) UEFA Super Cup
   b) UEFA Champions League
   c) UEFA Europa League

10. Which team in the Italian league is nicknamed 'La Vecchia Signora' which translates as 'the Old Lady'?
   a) AC Milan
   b) Napoli
   c) Juventus

11. Whose informal Barcelona contract was written on a napkin by Charly Rexach in December 2000?
   a) Luis Suárez
   b) Gerard Piquī
   c) Lionel Messi

12. After moving to Real Madrid, David Beckham chose jersey no. 23 because...
   a) Michael Jordan, his hero, wore it for the Chicago Bulls
   b) that is his birth date
   c) he was the 23rd player from England to play for the team

13. Which footballer was known as the 'fifth Beatle' because of his hair style?
   a) George Best
   b) Stanley Mathews
   c) Bobby Charlton

14. Who helped establish three football clubs in Durban, Pretoria and Johannesburg, all of which were named Passive Resisters Soccer Club?
   a) Nelson Mandela
   b) Martin Luther King Jr.
   c) Mahatma Gandhi

15. Instituted in 1888 in Shimla, it is the oldest football tournament in Asia and the third oldest football tournament in the world. Name it.
    a) IFA Shield
    b) Durand Cup
    c) Santosh Trophy

16. Who was the first Asian to score a hat-trick in football at the Olympics?
    a) P.K. Banerjee
    b) Neville D'Souza
    c) Sahu Mewalal

17. The Etihad Stadium is the home ground of which EPL team?
    a) Liverpool F.C.
    b) Manchester City
    c) Chelsea F.C.

18. Who replaced Ferenc Puskás as Europe's all-time top scorer, when he scored his 85th international goal at the FIFA World Cup 2018?
    a) Cristiano Ronaldo
    b) Harry Kane
    c) Romelu Lukaku

19. Who unintentionally hit David Beckham with a football boot in the dressing room, soon after which Beckham left Manchester United in 2003 to join Real Madrid?
    a) Wayne Rooney
    b) Paul Scholes
    c) Sir Alex Ferguson

20. In 2018, which Indian surpassed David Villa's record of 59 goals, making him the third highest scorer in terms of international goals?
    a) Bhaichung Bhutia
    b) Sunil Chhetri
    c) Gurpreet Singh Sandhu

SPORTY FACTS

▸ In 2018, FIFA World Cup 2018 topped the list of seaches on Google in India. The top three trending overall queries were: FIFA World Cup 2018, Live Score and IPL 2018.

▸ Cristiano Ronaldo's father was a big fan of Ronald Reagan, and so, he added the name Ronaldo to the name of his newborn son.

▸ In 1996, Shahid Afridi created a new record for the fastest one-day century when he scored a hundred off 37 balls against Sri Lanka. In his autobiography, *Game Changer*, he revealed that he had scored the century using Sachin Tendulkar's bat.

▸ The famous South Club in Kolkata is referred to as the 'cradle of tennis in India'.

▸ Paul '#Pogba' was the first Premier League player to have his own Twitter emoji.

GOLF

1. Who was the first player to successfully defend a Masters title?
   a) Tiger Woods
   b) Ben Hogan
   c) Jack Nicklaus

2. Who invented the golf club known as the sand wedge?
   a) Gary Player
   b) Gene Sarazen
   c) Sam Snead

3. Pantone 342 is the actual colour of the...
   a) Green jacket of Augusta
   b) Grass of Augusta National Golf Club
   c) Tennis ball used at the Augusta National Golf Club

4. Who is nicknamed 'Chipputtsia' because of his short game?
   a) Shubhankar Sharma
   b) S.S.P. Chawrasia
   c) Arjun Atwal

5. Which golfer said, 'This is a game of misses. The guy who misses the best is going to win'?
   a) Ben Hogan

    b)   Bobby Jones
    c)   Jack Nicklaus

6.   Who was the first player in the modern era to win four (modern-day) majors in succession?
    a)   Jack Nicklaus
    b)   Tiger Woods
    c)   Phil Mickleson

7.   What is a double eagle, a score of three strokes under par at a hole, also called?
    a)   Birdie
    b)   Albatross
    c)   Condor

8.   In 1960, why did Gary Player wear a pair of trousers with one black leg and one white leg to the Open Championship in St Andrews?
    a)   To advertise his new collection of trousers
    b)   He was the brand ambassador of Save the Zebra Foundation
    c)   To protest against apartheid

9.   In 1860, what was originally presented to the winner of the Open Championship?
    a)   A trophy
    b)   A belt
    c)   A crown

10.   Who among these had his golf balls painted black so he could still play when it snowed?
    a)   Woodrow Wilson

b) Donald Trump
c) Ronald Reagan

11. The famous golfer Vijay Singh was born in...
    a) Sri Lanka
    b) Fiji
    c) India

12. *Wonder Girl* is the biography of which famous golfer?
    a) Michelle Wie
    b) Annika Ṣṭrenstam
    c) Babe Didrikson Zaharias

13. In Switzerland, the first golf course, in Davos, was planned by which famous author?
    a) Arthur Conan Doyle
    b) Edgar Allan Poe
    c) Walt Whitman

14. Which word connects golf to a small tin in which tea is kept for daily use?
    a) Caddy
    b) Club
    c) Chest

15. In 1899, what was patented by George F. Grant, one of the first African American golfers?
    a) Tee
    b) Dimpled cover of the golf ball
    c) Golf cart

16. After World War I, the R&A enacted what is called

the '1.62 formula'. What did it standardize the size of?
a)   The hole
b)   The ball
c)   The club

17.   Which of these terms is used for an auction in which people bid on players or teams in a golf tournament?
a)   Bombay
b)   Calcutta
c)   Madras

18.   On 6 February 1971, who used a six-iron that he had smuggled on board Apollo 14, to hit two golf balls on the lunar surface, becoming the first person so far to play golf on the moon?
a)   Neil Armstrong
b)   Alan Shepard
c)   Edwin Aldrin

19.   With the signing of which treaty between England and Scotland was the ban on golf lifted in 1502?
a)   Treaty of Berlin
b)   Treaty of Edinburgh
c)   Treaty of Glasgow

20.   Who was the first sportsperson to receive three of the United States' civilian honours: the Presidential Medal of Freedom, the Congressional Gold Medal and the National Sports Award?
a)   Arnold Palmer
b)   Tiger Woods
c)   Jack Nicklaus

SPORTY FACTS

▸ Florence Griffith Joyner or Flo Jo, as she was popularly known, was the first American female Olympian to win four medals in a single year. She was famous not just for her sporting achievements but also for her long colourful fingernails.

▸ In 2018, Floyd Mayweather appeared on top of the list of the world's 100 highest-paid athletes by *Forbes* magazine.

▸ Geet Sethi was the first amateur to register an official maximum 147 break in a tournament in snooker.

▸ In Switzerland, a street leading to the national centre of Swiss tennis in Biel, is named after Roger Federer who trained there as a junior. It is now located on '1 Allīe Roger Federer'.

▸ In a fitting tribute to The Wall (Rahul Dravid), a wall of 10,000 bricks was constructed at the Chinnaswamy Stadium in Bengaluru in 2008. The number represented Dravid's 10,000-plus runs in both Test and ODIs.

HOCKEY

1. The word 'hockey' is said to have been derived from the French word meaning...
    a) Spade
    b) Goal
    c) Shepherd's crook

2. In hockey, what was introduced for the first time in the 1976 Montreal Olympics?
    a) Helmet for goalkeeper
    b) Suspension cards
    c) Artificial turf

3. The most goals scored by an individual in an Olympic men's hockey final is 5 by...
    a) Roop Singh
    b) Udham Singh
    c) Balbir Singh Sr.

4. In 2014, who became the co-owner of the Ranchi franchise of the Hero Hockey India League, 'Ranchi Rays'?
    a) M.S. Dhoni
    b) Deepika Kumari
    c) Manoj Bajpayee

5. The black disc made of hard rubber, used in ice hockey, is known as...

a) Hammer
b) Puck
c) Discus

6. In the history of hockey, why is Sansarpur, a village on the outskirts of Jalandhar, famous?
   a) It has the highest hockey ground in the world
   b) Hockey sticks were first produced in the village
   c) It has produced more than 8 Olympians for India.

7. In 1908, which team won the first ever gold medal for men's hockey at the Olympics?
   a) Ireland
   b) Great Britain
   c) Australia

8. The Sultan Azlan Shah Cup is named after HRH Sultan Azlan Shah, the ninth Yang di-Pertuan Agong (King) of…
   a) Sri Lanka
   b) Pakistan
   c) Malaysia

9. This Canadian ice-hockey player was nicknamed 'The Great One' because he was considered to be the greatest player in the history of the National Hockey League. The NHL retired his jersey number (99) after his final game. Who is he?
   a) Mark Messier
   b) Wayne Gretzky
   c) Sidney Crosby

10. In the Olympics, two Indians have won four individual medals in hockey. They are...
    a) Udham Singh and Leslie Claudius
    b) Dhyan Chand and Roop Singh
    c) Balbir Singh Sr. and Kishan Lal

11. Which was the first Indian city to host the Hockey World Cup?
    a) Kolkata
    b) Chennai
    c) Mumbai

12. Inaugurated in 1895, it is one of the oldest hockey tournaments in the world and is named after a legal remembrancer of the government of West Bengal. Name it.
    a) Stanley Cup
    b) Aga Khan Cup
    c) Beighton Cup

13. Which award is presented to FIH International Umpires who have completed their 100th official Senior International Inter Nations Match?
    a) Golden Card
    b) Golden Whistle
    c) Golden Cap

14. Leslie Claudius participated in four Olympic games and never returned empty-handed. He won three gold and a silver medals. According to him, the silver hurts because...
    a) He was the captain

b) He couldn't play the final match

c) They lost on penalties

15. Who was the captain of the Indian women's national hockey team in the film *Chak De! India*?
a) Vidya Sharma
b) Preety Sabharwal
c) Bindiya Naik

16. The Australia men's national field hockey team is popularly known as the...
a) Kangaroos
b) Kiwis
c) Kookaburras

17. During the 2012 London Olympics, after which famous hockey player was Watford High Street renamed?
a) Roop Singh
b) Dhanraj Pillay
c) Jaipal Singh

18. In the late 1980s, who is said to have first used the goal-scoring technique of 'drag-flick'?
a) Maurice Richard
b) Jay Stacy
c) Pargat Singh

19. Which sporting great said this about Dhyan Chand: 'He scores goals like runs in cricket'?
a) Donald Bradman
b) Pele
c) Jesse Owens

20. What was the contribution of Basheer Moojid of Pakistan to the world of hockey?
    a) He standardized the rules of hockey.
    b) He designed the trophy of the Hockey World Cup.
    c) He introduced the suspension cards.

SPORTY FACTS

▶ In F1 racing, drivers can lose around 2 to 4 kg of their body weight in a single race, because the heat in the cockpit causes a lot of water loss.

▶ In the Olympic Games, the apparatus used in rhythmic gymnastics like ropes, hoops, balls, clubs, and ribbons, can be of any colour except gold, silver and bronze.

▶ Bungee jumping is named after the strong cords that are normally used for securing luggage.

▶ In Ancient Egypt, one of the methods of weightlifting involved lifting a heavy sack of sand with one hand and keeping it high in a quasi-vertical position for a short period of time.

▶ Though cricket and football were popular in Bangladesh, Prime Minister Sheikh Mujibur Rahman, after independence, declared kabaddi as the national sport of the country.

INDIGENOUS GAMES

1. In which state did the martial art form Kalaripayattu originate?
   a) Kerala
   b) Manipur
   c) Maharashtra

2. The President's Trophy Boat Race, a popular snake boat racing event, is held at which lake?
   a) Vellayani Lake
   b) Ashtamudi lake
   c) Pookode Lake

3. It is said that in the ninteenth century, the British learned the nuances of the game of Sagol Kangjei from Manipur and after refinement called it...
   a) Football
   b) Hockey
   c) Polo

4. The name of which traditional sport of Tamil Nadu, celebrated on Mattu Pongal, comes from the Tamil words for 'coins' and 'package'?
   a) Asol Aap
   b) Jallikattu
   c) Onathallu

5. In ancient times, which game was known as 'rathera' as it was played on 'raths' or 'chariots'?
    a) Kho-kho
    b) Kangdi
    c) Sagol Kangjei

6. In which of the following traditional Indian sports do athletes perform a variety of yogic and gymnastic poses while suspended from a rope or pole?
    a) Mallakhamb
    b) Yubi Lakpi
    c) Vallamkali

7. Mukna is the Manipuri version of…
    a) Rugby
    b) Boxing
    c) Wrestling

8. If you were trying to catch a bunch of players while hopping on one leg, you would be playing….
    a) Langdi
    b) Kho-kho
    c) Kabaddi

9. Which of these is a traditional ball game played in Assam?
    a) Dhop Khel
    b) Khomlainai
    c) Teng Gooti

10. The name of which martial art form comes from the Tamil words for 'hill' and 'bamboo'?

a) Thangta
b) Silambam
c) Mukna

11. The winning pair of buffaloes in Kambala, a water buffalo race of southern India, was earlier awarded...
   a) A new shed
   b) A job with the local temple
   c) Coconuts and a bunch of plantains

12. Which traditional martial art form is historically associated with the Sikh gurus?
   a) Gatka
   b) Silambam
   c) Mallakhamb

13. Indigenous to Mizoram, Insuknawr is a game of...
   a) Football
   b) Boat racing
   c) Stick fighting

14. In the Manipuri game of Yubi Lakpi, what does the word 'Yubi' mean?
   a) Ball
   b) Coconut
   c) Kick

15. The traditional gym and training centre for Kushti, an ancient form of wrestling popular in India, is known as...
   a) Jhopri
   b) Maidan
   c) Akhara

16. The Kila Raipur Sports Festival, popularly known as India's 'Rural Olympics', is held in which state of India?
    a) Arunachal Pradesh
    b) Mahrashtra
    c) Punjab

17. If you take part in Asol Aap in the Nicobar islands, you would be participating in a/an...
    a) Boat race
    b) Archery competition
    c) Swimming competition

18. Since 1989, which city has hosted the International Kite Festival as part of the official celebration of Uttarayan?
    a) Kanpur
    b) Mumbai
    c) Ahmedabad

19. Amar, Sanjeevani and Gaminee are some of the styles of which of these games?
    a) Kho-kho
    b) Kabaddi
    c) Wrestling

20. Thoda, a traditional martial art form of Himachal Pradesh, displays one's skill in...
    a) Archery
    b) Wrestling
    c) Polo

SPORTY FACTS

▶ Tennis is said to have its origin in a French handball game called *jeu de paume,* meaning 'game of the palm'.

▶ According to a popular story, Christina Willes, sister of Kent cricketer John Willes, was responsible for the emergence of round-arm bowling. Originally, bowlers delivered the ball underarm. But Christina could not bowl underarm to John as her voluminous skirt came in the way. So she raised her arm higher than usual.

▶ Before the 2010 Commonwealth Games in New Delhi, more than 30 langurs were trained to curb the menace of food-snatching monkeys of the city.

▶ At the 2008 Beijing Games, Michael Phelps, the great swimmer, became the first athlete to win eight gold medals at a single Olympics.

▶ During his schooldays, Pele used to pronounce the name of the Vasco da Gama goalkeeper Bile as Pile. His classmates started calling him Pele and that name stuck.

INDIAN PREMIER LEAGUE

1. Who was the first captain to win the Orange Cap?
   a) David Warner
   b) Matthew Hayden
   c) Sachin Tendulkar

2. Who scored 158 runs against RCB in the first match of the inaugural IPL in 2008?
   a) Sourav Ganguly
   b) Brendon McCullum
   c) Graeme Smith

3. The 2009 edition of the IPL was held in South Africa because...
   a) The dates clashed with the Lok Sabha elections in India.
   b) Of prediction of a cyclone in India
   c) It was the centenary year of Nelson Mandela's birth.

4. Who said this about the IPL: 'It's like three-minute... noodles. Bang, bang, and it is over. For me, it is not cricket.'
   a) Arjuna Ranatunga
   b) Matthew Hayden
   c) Suresh Raina

5. How did Rohit Sharma get his nickname 'Hitman'?
   a) His favourite video game is Hitman.
   b) He was born in Pilib'hit'.
   c) He was referred to as 'Ro-Hit' by Ravi Shastri.

6. Who has captained the most number of matches in the history of the IPL?
   a) Virat Kohli
   b) Gautam Gambhir
   c) M.S. Dhoni

7. Tejashwi Yadav, son of Lalu Prasad Yadav, was a part of which IPL team in 2008?
   a) Kings XI Punjab
   b) Delhi Daredevils (renamed as Delhi Capitals)
   c) Mumbai Indians

8. National Award-winning music directors Aravind and Jaishankar composed 'Whistle Podu', the anthem of...
   a) Sunrisers Hyderabad
   b) Chennai Super Kings
   c) Royal Challengers Bangalore

9. In 2019, who became the first victim of 'mankading'?
   a) Shaun Marsh
   b) Hashim Amla
   c) Jos Buttler

10. What does 'Yatra Pratibha Avsara Prapnotihi', inscribed on the IPL trophy in Sanskrit, mean in English?

a) Where talent meets opportunity
b) Where ability meets agility
c) Where performance meets victory

11. Parthiv Patel is the first player in the IPL to...
    a) Hit a six
    b) Play for six different teams
    c) Be run-out

12. The logo of which team is inspired by the Sudarshan Chakra of Lord Krishna?
    a) Mumbai Indians
    b) Delhi Capitals
    c) Rajasthan Royals

13. Who was the first Indian to score a century in the IPL?
    a) Wriddhiman Saha
    b) Cheteshwar Pujara
    c) Manish Pandey

14. In 2019, a tweet from the official handle of which team read, 'Waste segregation makes recycling of waste simple. To raise awareness on recycling, the team wears green jerseys made of recycled plastic'?
    a) Royal Challengers Bangalore
    b) Mumbai Indians
    c) Chennai Super Kings

15. The year 2016 saw the introduction of which innovation conceived by an Australian mechanical

industrial designer named Bronte EcKermann to the league?
a) Snick-O-Meter
b) Hawk-Eye technology
c) LED stumps

16. As of 2019, who has hit the most number of sixes and is the first player to win the Orange Cap twice, consecutively, in 2011 and 2012?
a) Chris Gayle
b) Shaun Marsh
c) Matthew Hayden

17. Who coined the phrase '*Korbo, Lorbo, Jeetbo Re*' for the anthem of Kolkata Knight Riders?
a) Anik Dutta
b) Kaushik Ganguly
c) Sujoy Ghosh

18. Who sang the song 'Champion' at the opening ceremony of the 2016 edition of the IPL?
a) Chris Gayle
b) Dwayne Bravo
c) Dwayne Smith

19. In 2019, which team became the first to post 100 wins in the Indian Premier League?
a) Chennai Super Kings
b) Kolkata Knight Riders
c) Mumbai Indians

20. According to the rules of the IPL, what is the maximum number of overseas players each team can have on the field of play at any time during a match?

a) 4

b) 6

c) 8

SPORTY FACTS

▸ The Dronacharya Award is conferred on coaches who have successfully trained sportspersons and teams in India. The awardees receive a statuette of Guru Dronacharya, a certificate, ceremonial dress and a cash prize of five lakh rupees.

▸ Sepak Takraw, also known as kick volleyball, is a sport native to Southeast Asia. The objective in the sport is to volley a small ball over a five-foot-high net with any part of the body other than hands and arms.

▸ In chess, castling is a compound move of king and rook and is the only exception to the rule that a player may move only one piece at a time. It can be done no more than once in a game by each player.

▸ In sports, the term Cinderella story is used when an underdog—a person or a team—wins something, usually in a dramatic way.

▸ In 2000, when the MCC revised and re-wrote the Laws of Cricket, it included, for the first time, a Preamble on the Spirit of Cricket. The Preamble states: 'Cricket is a game that owes much of its unique appeal to the fact that it should be played not only within its Laws but also within the Spirit of the Game. Any action which is seen to abuse this Spirit causes injury to the game itself.'

MIXED BAG 1

1. Lansing State Journal sportswriter Fred Stabley Jr. was the first to...
    a) Call Earvin Johnson Jr. 'Magic'
    b) Give the name 'Dream Team' to the All Blacks
    c) Call Sachin Tendulkar 'the Little Master'

2. At the 1904 Olympic Games, which was the only official event in which women were allowed to contest?
    a) Archery
    b) Shooting
    c) Swimming

3. In which of these sports would the participants use a foil, an epee or a sabre?
    a) Fencing
    b) Archery
    c) Shooting

4. The sport Rugby is named after the famous Rugby School where the game was first played. In which country is it located?
    a) UK
    b) USA
    c) Canada

5. Who among these was not a part of the 1992

Basketball Dream Team?
a)   Shaquille O'Neal
b)   Charles Barkley
c)   Larry Bird

6.   Who was the first professional cricketer to be knighted?
a)   Douglas Jardine
b)   W.G. Grace
c)   Jack Hobbs

7.   Who was the first sportsperson to receive the Rajiv Gandhi Khel Ratna?
a)   Pankaj Advani
b)   Viswanathan Anand
c)   Leander Paes

8.   The name of which game is derived from a Swahili word which means 'to build'?
a)   Jenga
b)   Shogi
c)   Mancala

9.   In May 1997, who was defeated by Deep Blue, a computer developed by IBM?
a)   Garry Kasparov
b)   Viswanathan Anand
c)   Vladimir Kramnik

10. In which city is the Bird's Nest stadium located?
a)   Beijing
b)   Milan
c)   London

11. Whose autobiography is titled *A Shot at History: My Obsessive Journey to Olympic Gold*?
    a) Abhinav Bindra
    b) Michael Phelps
    c) Usain Bolt

12. Which of these games was originally nicknamed 'whiff-whaff'?
    a) Badminton
    b) Polo
    c) Table tennis

13. With which sport would you associate Simona Amanar, Natalia Yurchenko and Mitsuo Tsukahara?
    a) Artistic gymnastics
    b) Figure skating
    c) Diving

14. Which famous fictional character is said to have been named after a Nottinghamshire cricketer?
    a) Sherlock Holmes
    b) Captain Ahab
    c) David Copperfield

15. Which is the oldest sport on the Olympic Winter Games programme?
    a) Ice hockey
    b) Figure skating
    c) Ski jumping

16. Who was the first person to ever win an NBA Most Valuable Player award, an NBA Coach of the Year

award and an NBA Executive of the Year award?
a) Kareem Abdul-Jabbar
b) Larry Bird
c) Magic Johnson

17. In 2017, who surpassed Michael Jordan as the NBA's all-time playoff scoring leader with 5,995 points, a record held by Michael Jordan for 20 years?
a) Kobe Bryant
b) Le Bron James
c) James Harden

18. Which sport is nicknamed 'the roaring game' because of the rumbling sound the 19.96 kg granite stones make when they travel across the ice?
a) Curling
b) Ice hockey
c) Figure skating

19. The Venus Rosewater Dish is awarded in which sport?
a) Cricket
b) Football
c) Tennis

20. Which of these was established in 1903 by Henri Desgrange to boost the circulation of his newspaper *L'Auto*, now known as *L'Equipe*?
a) Tour de France
b) Daytona 500
c) World Rally Championship

SPORTY FACTS

▸ In 1974, in a match at Edgbaston, Ashok Mankad's cap fell on to the stumps and dislodged the bails as he faced a bouncer from Chris Old. Verdict: Out!

▸ According to Hookit, Cristiano Ronaldo was the first sportsperson to reach 200 million combined followers across Twitter, Instagram and Facebook.

▸ The Four Musketeers of France—Rene Lacoste, Jean Borotra, Henri Cochet and Jacques Brugnon—won every Davis Cup between 1927 and 1932.

▸ 5 February is celebrated as Shahid Afridi Day in the city of Port Arthur, Texas.

▸ Asian Games gold medallist Hima Das is popularly known as the Dhing Express.

1. In 2017, after which sportsperson was Madeira airport in Portugal renamed?
   a) Cristiano Ronaldo
   b) Luís Figo
   c) Luís Nani

2. He was swapped with another newborn by mistake. His uncle had seen a small hole in his ear and noticed that the hole was missing in the child the following day. The infant was finally found sleeping beside a fisherwoman. Who is he?
   a) Sachin Tendulkar
   b) Sunil Gavaskar
   c) Ajinkya Rahane

3. In which sport do players use a staff that is sharply bent at the top to form a hook and a ball made of sponge rubber, about 20 cm in circumference?
   a) Lacrosse
   b) Golf
   c) Polo

4. Which is the slowest competitive stroke in swimming?
   a) Breaststroke
   b) Backstroke
   c) Butterfly

5. Which Olympic sport has sweep and sculling events?
   a) Rowing
   b) Cycling
   c) Boxing

6. Which sport was originally called mintonette?
   a) Volleyball
   b) Basketball
   c) Rugby

7. In 1985, Michael Jordan was fined $5,000 for every game that he played because of an article he wore that violated NBA league policy. What was the article of controversy?
   a) His headgear
   b) His jersey
   c) His sneakers

8. Who is the only sportsperson to have won the Rajiv Gandhi Khel Ratna for contribution to two sports disciplines?
   a) Geet Sethi
   b) Abhinav Bindra
   c) Pankaj Advani

9. With which athlete would you associate the book *Beneath the Surface*?
   a) Mark Spitz
   b) Michael Phelps
   c) Matt Biondi

10. In Japanese, the name of this sport means 'the way of suppleness'. The rules of this sport were codified by Dr Jigoro Kano. Name the sport.
    a) Judo
    b) Tae kwon do
    c) Karate

11. In the Olympics, which sport has events like Slalom, Giant Slalom and Downhill?
    a) Alpine skiing
    b) Ice hockey
    c) Figure skating

12. Which of these words comes from an ancient Greek word for 'one who competes for a prize'?
    a) Champion
    b) Amateur
    c) Athlete

13. In which sport is the scrum a way of re-starting play?
    a) Football
    b) Basketball
    c) Rugby

14. Along with Jacques Levy, who co-wrote the lyrics of 'Hurricane', a song about the trial and tribulations of boxer Ruben Carter?
    a) Bob Dylan
    b) John Stewart
    c) Eric Clapton

15. Which sport was invented by James W. Naismith, an instructor at the YMCA Training School in Massachusetts, to keep his students fit and warm during the cold winters?
    a) Football
    b) Basketball
    c) Badminton

16. In which country is the Cresta Run, a 1,213-metre course from St. Moritz to the town of Celerin, located?
    a) Switzerland
    b) Sweden
    c) Finland

17. According to whose final wishes was his body buried at the Bois de Vaux cemetery in Lausanne, but his heart sent to Olympia, where it is kept in a marble monument?
    a) Jesse Owens
    b) Pierre de Coubertin
    c) Paavo Nurmi

18. Which sport uses a ball 40 mm in diameter, weighing 2.7 g and made of plastic?
    a) Tennis
    b) Cricket
    c) Table Tennis

19. Luge is the French word for...
    a) Sledge
    b) Skeleton
    c) Snow

20. The name of which martial art was officially adopted in 1955 after it was submitted by Choi Hong-Hi, its principal founder?
    a) Tae kwon do
    b) Karate
    c) Sumo

SPORTY FACTS

▸ During the 2017 Women's World Cup, #MithaliRaj was the most used hashtag emoji on the Twitter Emoji Leaderboard.

▸ After watching Chris Gayle dance after the World Twenty20 win in 2012, 'Zinga', a dance artist and former cricketer, created a 'Chris Gayle Cover Drive' dance.

▸ During the victory ceremony at the 1968 Olympic Games in Mexico City, the winners of the gold and bronze medals in the men's 200 m run, American sprinters Tommie Smith and John Carlos, stood on the medal podium, bowed their heads and raised black-gloved fists during the national anthem. Referred to as the Black Power salute, it was their way of paying tribute to their African American heritage and protesting against the poor living conditions of the minorities in the USA. Fallout: Both of them were banned from the Olympics for life.

▶ In cricket, the term 'doosra' was first used for an unconventional off-spin delivery by Pakistani spinner Saqlain Mushtaq in a match against Australia in the Sharjah series. This invention was named 'doosra' by Saqlain Mushtaq's team-mate Moin Khan. Interestingly, the term 'teesra', used for another unconventional off-spin delivery, is called a 'jalebi'!

▶ Naomi Osaka shares her surname with the city of her birth, Osaka, Japan.

MIXED BAG 3

1. Who did Eddie Paynter replace on the list of players named for the Ashes tour in 1932-33?
    a) Nawab of Pataudi
    b) Duleepsinhji
    c) Ranjeetsinhji

2. Mrs Brohy and Miss Ohnier were the first women to compete in the modern Olympic Games. Which sport did they compete in?
    a) Croquet
    b) Tennis
    c) Polo

3. Along with Jacques Levy, who co-wrote the lyrics of 'Hurricane', a song about the trial and imprisonment of boxer Ruben Carter?
    a) Bob Dylan
    b) John Stewart
    c) Eric Clapton

4. What is Silvio Gazzaniga's contribution to the FIFA World Cup?
    a) He was the first match referee.
    b) He designed the first mascot.
    c) He designed the new trophy.

5. Who holds the record for most games played at the

FIFA World Cup?
a)   Paolo Maldini
b)   Lothar Matthaeus
c)   Diego Maradona

6.   In 2005, at Trent Bridge, the ball Chris Tremlett bowled to Mohammad Ashraful landed on the top of the middle stump but did not dislodge the bails. What was the decision of the umpire?
a)   The batsman was given 'not out'.
b)   It was declared a dead ball.
c)   The batsman was given out.

7.   Until Michael Phelps broke the record in London, this athlete was the only person in any sport to have won eighteen Olympic medals. Name this athlete.
a)   Larissa Latynina
b)   Wilma Rudolph
c)   Carl Lewis

8.   Captain Roop Singh Stadium in Gwalior is named after the younger brother of which famous sportsperson?
a)   Milkha Singh
b)   Dhyan Chand
c)   K.D. Jadhav

9.   Tiger Woods called this golfer 'the grandfather I never had'. Who was he talking about?
a)   Arnold Palmer
b)   Jack Nicklaus
c)   Charlie Sifford

10. Which film, directed by Brian Helgeland, is also the jersey number worn by baseball player Jackie Robinson?
    a) 42
    b) 32
    c) 4

11. Rich Uncle Pennybags is the mascot of which board game?
    a) Monopoly
    b) Scrabble
    c) Backgammon

12. Who was the director of MVP: Most Valuable Primate, a film about an ape playing sports?
    a) Robert Vince
    b) Ridley Scott
    c) Peter Jackson

13. The first time women competed in pentathlon was in 1964, at the Olympic Games in Tokyo. This format was later replaced by the heptathlon, with the addition of the 800 m sprint and...
    a) Javelin throw
    b) Hammer throw
    c) Race walking

14. 'The Races at Longchamps', a painting depicting a horse race, is a work by which famous painter?
    a) Edouard Manet
    b) Claude Monet
    c) Henri Rousseau

15. Which cricketer holds the record for the longest Test career?
    a) Hanif Mohammad
    b) Wilfred Rhodes
    c) Sachin Tendulkar

16. In the Persian game hokm, the aim of the game is to get...
    a) Seven points
    b) Ten points
    c) Eleven points

17. Which famous film was inspired by a match between Muhammad Ali and Chuck Wepner on 24 March 1975 in Richfield, Ohio?
    a) *Rocky*
    b) *The Wrestler*
    c) *Raging Bull*

18. In 1977, which of these won the Grammy Award in the Best Instrumental Arrangement category?
    a) *Nadia's Theme*
    b) *Time to Shine*
    c) *We Stand Together*

19. What kind of an animal was World Cup Willie, the first official mascot of FIFA?
    a) Zebra
    b) Lion
    c) Armadillo

20. Who was the first professional cricketer to be knighted?
    a) Douglas Jardine
    b) W.G. Grace
    c) Jack Hobbs

SPORTY FACTS

▸ Rajyavardhan Singh Rathore, who won India's first individual Olympic silver medal at the Athens 2004 Olympic Games, was appointed as the Minister of State (Independent Charge), Ministry of Youth Affairs and Sports, in 2017.

▸ Luka Modric, Real Madrid and Croatia midfielder, won the 2018 Ballon d'Or, becoming the first player other than Lionel Messi or Cristiano Ronaldo to win the award in a decade.

▸ In 2011, M.S. Dhoni was conferred the honorary rank of Lieutenant Colonel for his contribution to cricket. Sachin Tendulkar joined the Indian Air Force with the rank of group captain.

▸ Michael Schumacher provided the voice of a Ferrari in the 2006 film *Cars*.

▸ In the 1920s, Johnny Weissmuller, an American swimmer, won five gold medals at the Olympic Games and set numerous world records. Though this was no mean achievement, he is chiefly remembered for his role as Tarzan in *Tarzan of the Apes* and in more than ten Tarzan films that followed.

OLYMPIC GAMES

1. The 2012 London Games were the first Olympics in which...
   a) The winter and summer games were contested simultaneously
   b) All participating countries sent female athletes
   c) The Olympic flame was not lit

2. What was Father Henri Didon's contribution to the Olympic Games?
   a) The Olympic motto
   b) The Olympic flag
   c) The Olympic torch

3. In 1924, the Olympic marathon distance was standardized at 42,195 m based on a decision of the British Olympic Committee to start the 1908 Olympic race from Windsor Castle and finish it...
   a) At the centre of the stadium
   b) In front of the royal box in the stadium
   c) In front of the Olympic torch

4. Who wrote the poem 'Ode to Sport' under the pseudonyms George Hohrod and Martin Eschbach for the 1912 Stockholm Games?
   a) Jules Rimet
   b) Baron Pierre de Coubertin
   c) Jim Thorpe

5. Why was champion swimmer Dawn Fraser banned from competitions for many years?
   a) For allegedly stealing a flag from the Japanese Imperial Palace
   b) For testing positive for drugs
   c) For participating as a man

6. King Constantine, who won a gold medal for sailing at the 1960 Rome Olympics, was the king of...
   a) Greece
   b) Spain
   c) Italy

7. Which sportsperson is nicknamed 'The Baltimore Bullet' and the 'Flying Fish'?
   a) Mark Spitz
   b) Michael Phelps
   c) Ian Thorpe

8. Which sport, last played at the 1904 Summer Olympics, was re-introduced after 112 years at the 2016 Rio Olympics?
   a) Basketball
   b) Badminton
   c) Golf

9. In which of these sports do men and women compete against each other on equal terms?
   a) Football
   b) Hockey
   c) Equestrian

10. In AD 67, who is said to have paid off everyone so he wouldn't have to actually compete against anyone and went on to win olive wreaths in the chariot race?
    a) Julius Caesar
    b) Emperor Nero
    c) Caligula

11. The 1904 Olympic Games in St Louis were the first at which...
    a) The Olympic flag was used
    b) Gold, silver and bronze medals were awarded
    c) The Closing Ceremony was held

12. Which is the first city to have hosted both the Asian Games and the Olympic Games?
    a) Tokyo
    b) Seoul
    c) Beijing

13. Which member of Emperor Haile Selassie's bodyguard ran barefoot at the 1960 Olympic Games in Rome and won a gold medal in Marathon?
    a) Larbi Bouraada
    b) Chioma Ajunwa
    c) Abebe Bikila

14. Aerials and Moguls are events of which sport in the Winter Olympics?
    a) Freestyle skiing
    b) Bobsleigh
    c) Curling

15. In 1976, in Montreal, she became the first gymnast in Olympic history to be awarded the perfect score of 10.0 for her performance on the uneven bars. She went on to record the perfect 10.0 six more times and became the youngest all-around Olympic gold medalist.
    a) Nadia Comaneci
    b) Nastia Liukin
    c) Shawn Johnson

16. A refugee team took part in the Olympic Games for the first time in 2016. The Refugee Olympic Team comprised 10 athletes hailing from South Sudan, the Democratic Republic of Congo, Ethiopia and...
    a) Somalia
    b) Eritiea
    c) Syria

17. K.D. Jadav, who was the first Indian to win an Olympic medal (bronze) in an individual sport, won his medal in which sport?
    a) Wrestling
    b) Archery
    c) Swimming

18. In 1928, the Indian hockey team won their first Olympic gold medal by defeating which team?
    a) USA
    b) Hungary
    c) The Netherlands

19. Who won the first individual gold medal for India at the Olympics?
    a) Rajyavardhan Singh Rathore
    b) Vijay Kumar
    c) Abhinav Bindra

20. The first Olympic medal for Ireland was for…
    a) Painting
    b) Swimming
    c) Architecture

SPORTY FACTS

▸ According to Hindu mythology, Arjuna was a great archer. One day, Dronacharya, the teacher of the Kauravas and Pandavas, decided to test the skills of his students. He placed a wooden bird on a tree and asked his students to describe what they saw. All, except Arjuna, described the surroundings along with the bird. Only Arjuna said that he saw only the bird and was successful in hitting the target.

▸ Vladimir Putin, President of Russia, was awarded a ninth Dan ranking in Taekwondo by the World Taekwondo Federation in 2013.

▸ In baseball, if a pitcher faces 27 batters and none of them get on base, it is referred to as a perfect game.

▸ Chess has often been referred to as the 'royal game' because of its association with the nobility.

▸ In 1999, Muhammad Ali was named BBC Sports Personality of the Century.

ONE DAY INTERNATIONALS AND THE WORLD CUP

1. Each innings of the first ODI match ever played consisted of how many overs?
    a) 40
    b) 50
    c) 60

2. First held in 2011, the 'Pink ODI' was so called because it was played...
    a) With a pink ball
    b) To raise awareness about breast cancer
    c) Played in Jaipur

3. In ODIs, who has played the most number of matches as captain?
    a) M.S. Dhoni
    b) Ricky Ponting
    c) A. Ranatunga

4. What connects K.C. Wessels, X.M. Marshall, L. Ronchi and A.C. Cummins?
    a) They have represented two countries in ODIs.
    b) They captained their side on their debut.
    c) They did not get the opportunity to bat in ODIs.

5. A sponsor of the 2007 World Cup donated US$ 1 million to charity when Herschelle Gibbs achieved

which feat at the tournament?
a) Hit six sixes in an over
b) Became the only batsman to be not out
c) Scored the fastest century

6. Who is the only Indian to be dismissed for handling
    the ball and obstructing the field in ODIs?
    a) Kapil Dev
    b) Vijay Hazare
    c) Mohinder Amarnath

7. In 1971, before the first match in ODI history, who
    said to the crowds, 'You have seen history made'?
    a) Don Bradman
    b) Ashley Mallett
    c) Douglas Jardine

8. At the 2003 World Cup, who bowled the first
    recorded ball to offically pass the 100 mph mark?
    a) Shoaib Akhtar
    b) Brett Lee
    c) Lasith Malinga

9. Spanning 22 years 91 days, which cricketer has had
    one of the longest careers in ODIs?
    a) Sanath Jayasuriya
    b) Sachin Tendulkar
    c) Wasim Akram

10. In the history of ODIs, who was the first batsman to
    be given out LBW by a third umpire?
    a) Shoaib Malik

    b)   Sachin Tendulkar
    c)   Carl Hooper

11.   Which Indian has taken 334 wickets in ODIs, the most by an Indian?
    a)   Harbhajan Singh
    b)   Anil Kumble
    c)   Kapil Dev

12.   Who faced the first ball in the history of ODIs?
    a)   Ian Chappell
    b)   Allan Border
    c)   Geoffrey Boycott

13.   Who is the first female bowler to take 200 wickets in ODIs?
    a)   Jhulan Goswami
    b)   Jess Jonassen
    c)   Marizanne Kapp

14.   Who holds the record for the most number of ODI centuries among Indian captains?
    a)   M.S. Dhoni
    b)   Virat Kohli
    c)   Sourav Ganguly

15.   In a 1992 ODI match against South Africa, who was 'mankaded' by Kapil Dev?
    a)   Jonty Rhodes
    b)   Allan Donald
    c)   Peter Kirsten

16.   Who is the only player to win four consecutive Man-

of-the-Match awards in ODIs?

a)   A.B. de Villiers

b)   Sourav Ganguly

c)   Andrew Flintoff

17.   Who was the first bowler to take three hat-tricks in ODIs?

a)   Brett Lee

b)   Wasim Akram

c)   Lasith Malinga

18.   On his debut, Sachin Tendulkar was the second youngest debutant at 16 years, 238 days. Who was the only cricketer to have made his ODI debut at a younger age till then?

a)   Hasan Raza

b)   Aaqib Javed

c)   Haseeb Hameed

19.   Who is the first non-Australian captain to win 100 ODI matches?

a)   M.S. Dhoni

b)   Andrew Strauss

c)   Graeme Smith

20.   How many runs did Gary Sobers score in his only ODI?

a)   Zero

b)   A century

c)   13

SPORTY FACTS

▸ In 1968, Billie Jean King received £750 after winning at Wimbledon. Her male counterpart Rod Laver, on the other hand, received £2,000.

▸ Kendo, a traditional Japanese style of fencing, is widely practised by the police and the armed forces of Japan.

▸ Long before *Lagaan* and *Dangal*, Aamir Khan played a sportsperson in the 1990 film *Awwal Number*. Centred on cricket, this film was directed by Dev Anand.

▸ Deli Singh Rana, known as The Great Khali in the WWE circuit, is said to have derived his ring name from Goddess Kali.

▸ Jonty Rhodes, the former South African cricketer, named his daughter India, after the country of her birth.

SPORTS AND ANIMALS

1. What does the word Buzkashi, an important sport of Afghanistan, mean?
    a) Goat dragging
    b) Bull fighting
    c) Cock fighting

2. A game in which sport consists of six periods of 7 1/2 minutes each, called chukkers?
    a) Polo
    b) Bull fighting
    c) Horse racing

3. The modern form of which sport has its origins in the streets of medieval England where the object was to drag a pig's bladder to markers at either end of town?
    a) Football
    b) Hockey
    c) Basketball

4. Which of these animals had successfully predicted a FIFA World Cup winner?
    a) Paul the Octopus
    b) Peter the Tortoise
    c) Elephant Nelly

5. What was discovered by Pickles, a collie, on his daily

walk on 27 March 1966?
a) Jules Rimet Trophy
b) Jesse Owens' gold medal
c) Baron de Coubertin's tomb

6. Peter the Cat is the first animal to...
a) Be hired by Lord's to keep birds off the field
b) Get a mention in the Wisden Cricketers' Almanack
c) Become the mascot of the Commonwealth Games

7. Which king died of injuries received in a polo match?
a) Qutb ud Din Aibak
b) Tipu Sultan
c) Akbar

8. What does the word 'Dressage' mean in French?
a) Training
b) Jumping
c) Galloping

9. At the entrance to Las Ventas bullring in Madrid you would come across a bronze figure of a matador saluting the bust of a famous scientist for saving the lives of so many bullfighters. Who is the scientist?
a) Louis Pasteur
b) Alexander Fleming
c) Edward Jenner

10. Which of these gets its name from races by fox hunters in Ireland over natural country in which

churches served as course landmarks?

a) Steeplechasing
b) Dressage
c) Rodeo

11. What kind of a creature was Waldi, the mascot of the first Olympic Games?

a) Dog
b) Bear
c) Lion

12. Which book by Laura Hillenbrand was made into a film by Gary Ross?

a) *The Call of the Wild*
b) *Seabiscuit: An American Legend*
c) *White Fang*

13. In cricket, which term was first used in a newspaper report about a cricket match played by the Prince of Wales (the future Edward VII) on 17 July 1866?

a) Duck
b) Rabbit
c) Cow corner

14. In which sport do competitors wear skis and clutch reins attached to a wooden harness fitted onto one or more horses, ponies or dogs?

a) Skijoring
b) Luge
c) Sledding

15. At the 1932 Olympic Games, which were the only two countries that participated in Sled Dog Racing?
    a) Canada and USA
    b) Sweden and The Netherlands
    c) UK and Finland

16. Rufus the Hawk succeeded Hamish as the official...
    a) Bird scarer at Wimbledon
    b) Burrow spotter at Old Trafford
    c) Carcass remover at Lord's

17. Which sport has two main forms: tudabaray and qarajay?
    a) Buzkashi
    b) Jallikattu
    c) Sepak Takraw

18. The earliest account of what occurs in Homer's description of the funeral of Patroclus?
    a) Chariot race
    b) Cockfighting
    c) Bullfighting

19. Sabong is a popular pastime in the Philippines. It is another name for...
    a) Polo
    b) Camel racing
    c) Cockfighting

20. In which sport would you use an eyas, a passager and a haggard?

a) Pigeon shooting
b) Camel racing
c) Falconry

SPORTY FACTS

▸ In China, the ninth day of the ninth month is celebrated as Kites' Day, or the Festival for Climbing Heights. It is a holiday honouring kites.

▸ In 2018, India became the first country to win the U-19 cricket World Cup four times. India won its first title in 2000, under the captainship of Muhammad Kaif.

▸ The mascot of the 1982 FIFA World Cup was an orange named Naranjito and the one for the 1986 Mexico event was a hot pepper named Pique.

▸ In 2007, Roger Federer became the first living Swiss person to appear on a postage stamp in Switzerland.

▸ Esports, a form of competition using video games, appeared as a demonstration event at the 2018 Asian Games held in Indonesia. Players competed in six video games: League of Legends, PES 2018, StarCraft 2, Hearthstone, Arena of Valor and Clash Royale.

TENNIS

1. Who wrote in his autobiography, 'It's no accident, I think, that tennis uses the language of life. Advantage, service, fault, break, love, the basic elements of tennis are those of everyday existence, because every match is a life in miniature'?
   a) Andre Agassi
   b) Rafael Nadal
   c) Serena Williams

2. Who defeated Bobby Riggs in an exhibition match dubbed the 'Battle of the Sexes'?
   a) Martina Navratilova
   b) Margaret Court
   c) Billie Jean King

3. Who was the first Indian player to win the boys' singles title at Wimbledon?
   a) Vijay Amritraj
   b) Ramanathan Krishnan
   c) Leander Paes

4. In 1932, this player decided to do away with the flannel trousers that the players of the day wore and became the first person to play a Wimbledon match in a pair of shorts. Name him.
   a) Fred Perry
   b) Don Budge
   c) Bunny Austin

5. Who is the first female tennis player to receive the Rajiv Gandhi Khel Ratna award?
   a) Sania Mirza
   b) Kiran Bedi
   c) Nirupama Mankad

6. Which invention by James Van Alen was adopted by the U.S. Open in 1970 to speed up the game?
   a) Deuce
   b) Double fault
   c) Tiebreak

7. Which tennis player's mother participated in the 1972 Summer Olympic Games in basketball?
   a) Leander Paes
   b) Andre Agassi
   c) Pete Sampras

8. This sportsperson received a cow as gift in 2003 and named her Juliet. He was honoured with another cow in 2013 whom he named Desiree. Name this sportsperson.
   a) Rafael Nadal
   b) Roger Federer
   c) Novak Djokovic

9. *You Cannot Be Serious* is a book by which tennis star?
   a) John McEnroe
   b) Boris Becker
   c) Jimmy Connors

10. An extract from whose poem is used as a quotation at the entrance to the centre court at Wimbledon?
    a) Rudyard Kipling
    b) William Wordsworth
    c) Alfred Tennyson

11. Which Grand Slam was played on grass from 1881 to 1974, and on clay from 1975 to 1977, and has been played on DecoTurf since then?
    a) US Open
    b) Wimbledon
    c) French Open

12. Who is the first player to complete the 'Golden Grand Slam' in a single year?
    a) Venus Williams
    b) Steffi Graf
    c) Maria Sharapova

13. Who, along with Liz Nickles, wrote a series of mysteries featuring Jordan Myles, a former tennis champion turned sleuth?
    a) Chris Evert
    b) Martina Navratilova
    c) Margaret Court

14. In a match, zero is called 'love', which is derived from the French word for what?
    a) Egg
    b) Orange
    c) Peach

15. Jimmy Connors once said, '[In the modern game], you're a clay-court specialist, a grass-court specialist or a hard-court specialist...or you're _____ _____.'
    a) Andre Agassi
    b) Rod Laver
    c) Roger Federer

16. In tennis, if you won the Channel Slam, you would be...
    a) A British player who has won the French Open.
    b) A player who has won the French Open and Wimbledon back-to-back.
    c) A French player who has won Wimbledon.

17. Melanie Molitor, a tennis player herself, named her daughter after one of the greatest tennis players of all time. What did she call her?
    a) Martina Hingis
    b) Maria Sharapova
    c) Petra Kvitova

18. In which work by Shakespeare does the Dauphin, the son of the king of France, send a contemptuous gift of a container of tennis balls?
    a) Henry V
    b) Julius Caesar
    c) King Lear

19. Which country did India play in the finals of the Davis Cup in 1966?
    a) Australia

   b)   West Germany
   c)   Romania

20. In 1972, the International Tennis Federation
    introduced yellow tennis balls into the rules of
    tennis. Why was it changed?
    a)   It was the colour of the British monarchy.
    b)   It was more restful for the players.
    c)   It was more visible to television viewers.

INSPIRATIONAL QUOTES
BY SPORTSPERSONS

▸ 'Champions keep playing until they get it right.'
                                    —Billie Jean King

▸ 'If you fail to prepare, you're prepared to fail.'
                                    —Mark Spitz

▸ 'Persistence can change failure into extraordinary
  achievement.'

                                    —Matt Biondi

▸ 'You are never really playing an opponent. You are
  playing yourself, your own highest standards, and
  when you reach your limits, that is real joy.'
                                    —Arthur Ashe

▸ 'What makes something special is not just what you
  have to gain, but what you feel there is to lose.'
                                    —Andre Agassi

▸ 'The more difficult the victory, the greater the happiness in winning.'

—Pele

▸ 'One man can be a crucial ingredient on a team, but one man cannot make a team.'

—Kareem Abdul-Jabbar

▸ 'You've got to take the initiative and play your game. In a decisive set, confidence is the difference.'

—Chris Evert

TEST CRICKET

1. The BCCI initially wanted to make the Freedom Trophy, that is awarded to the winner of the Mahatma Gandhi-Nelson Mandela series, with what?
    a) Prison rods of the cells of the two leaders
    b) Soil from the prisons they spent time in
    c) Their ashes

2. What was the colour of the ball used in the first day-night Test match?
    a) Red
    b) White
    c) Pink

3. Who was the first cricketer to score a century in Test cricket?
    a) Charles Bannerman
    b) Don Bradman
    c) W.G. Grace

4. Which Test cricketer lent his name to a form of dismissal in which a bowler takes off the bails in his delivery stride if the batsman at the non-striker's end walks out of his crease?
    a) Lala Amarnath
    b) Vinoo Mankad
    c) Javed Miandad

5. Who left in the middle of a 1983 Test and rushed from Antigua to Barbados on hearing the news of his ailing daughter, making him the only batsman to be 'retired not out' till then?
    a) Vivian Richards
    b) Curtly Ambrose
    c) Gordon Greenidge

6. Who was the first Hindu to play Test cricket for Pakistan?
    a) Danish Kaneria
    b) Anil Dalpat
    c) Rohan Kanhai

7. Which is the only team to beat England in their first ever tour to England?
    a) India
    b) Pakistan
    c) Sri Lanka

8. Who is the first batsman to hit a six off the first ball of a Test match?
    a) Yuvraj Singh
    b) Chris Gayle
    c) Sachin Tendulkar

9. If M.L. Jaisimha and Ravi Shastri were the first two, who was the third Indian to bat on all five days of a Test match?
    a) Manoj Tiwari
    b) Cheteshwar Pujara
    c) V.V.S. Laxman

10. Who is the only bowler to dismiss Don Bradman hit wicket in Test cricket?
    a) Harold Larwood
    b) Lala Amarnath
    c) H.Verity

11. Which cricketer was so happy with his score of 277 at the SCG in 1993 that he named his first daughter after the city?
    a) Brian Lara
    b) Ricky Ponting
    c) Shane Warne

12. Who said, 'When I win the toss on a good pitch, I bat. When I win the toss on a doubtful pitch, I think about it a bit and then I bat. When I win the toss on a very bad pitch, I think about it a bit longer and then I bat'?
    a) W.G. Grace
    b) Donald Bradman
    c) Garfield Sobers

13. Who is the first bowler to take a hat-trick in the very first over of a Test match?
    a) Dale Steyn
    b) Brett Lee
    c) Irfan Pathan

14. The record partnership by siblings in Tests stands at 269 which was created by...
    a) Ian and Greg Chappell
    b) Grant and Andy Flower

c) Mark and Steve Waugh

15. Virender Sehwag is the first Indian to score a triple century in Test cricket. Who is the second?
a) Karun Nair
b) Virat Kohli
c) Rohit Sharma

16. In 1955, against which team did New Zealand score 26 runs in a Test innings, the lowest total to ever be scored in a Test match so far?
a) England
b) India
c) Pakistan

17. The match popularly referred to as the 'Timeless Test' spanned from 3 March to 14 March 1939 and was played between England and...
a) South Africa
b) West Indies
c) Australia

18. Who is the only Test player to have played for both India and England?
a) Roger Binny
b) Farokh Engineer
c) Iftikhar Ali Khan Pataudi

19. Who finished with 998 international dismissals as a wicketkeeper, but only one Test wicket, that of Dwayne Bravo, as a bowler?
a) Adam Gilchrist

    b)   Mark Boucher
    c)   Ian Healy

20. When the Laws of Cricket were redrafted in 2017, two laws were deleted. If one was 'Handled the ball', which was the other?
    a)   Lost ball
    b)   Timed out
    c)   Stumped

INSPIRATIONAL QUOTES BY SPORTSPERSONS

▶ 'The mind is the limit. As long as the mind can envision the fact that you can do something, you can do it, as long as you really believe 100 per cent.'

—Arnold Schwarzenegger

▶ 'When I go out there, I have no pity on my brother. I am out there to win.'

—Joe Frazier

▶ 'You have to expect things of yourself before you can do them.'

—Michael Jordan

▶ 'Pain is temporary. It may last a minute, or an hour, or a day, or a year, but eventually it will subside and something else will take its place. If I quit, however, it lasts forever.'

—Lance Armstrong

▶ 'It doesn't matter what your background is and where you come from, if you have dreams and goals, that's all that matters.'

—Serena Williams

▶ 'The important thing in the Olympic Games is to participate. The most important thing in life is not to win in spite of everything. The most important subject is having struggled in the best way. If we spread this and have this adopted as necessary, we shall have created a more powerful, more courageous and most important of all, more ethical and more generous mankind.'

—Baron Pierre de Coubertin

▶ 'Impossible is just a big word thrown around by small men who find it easier to live in the world they've been given than to explore the power they have to change it. Impossible is not a fact. It's an opinion. Impossible is not a declaration. It's a dare. Impossible is potential. Impossible is temporary. Impossible is nothing.'

—Muhammad Ali

▶ 'Be the hardest working person you can be. That's how you separate yourself from the competition.'

—Stephen Curry

ANSWERS

ASHES

1. He wrote a mock obituary giving rise to the legend
2. Terracotta
3. Graham Gooch
4. Sharne Warne
5. An actual trophy
6. Shane Warne's first delivery in Ashes in 1993
7. Ian Botham
8. Douglas Jardine
9. Marylebone Cricket Club
10. Don Bradman
11. Ivo
12. Compton-Miller Medal
13. Steve Waugh
14. Remains of her mother-in-law's veil
15. R.M. Crockett
16. To play each innings on a separate pitch
17. Bill Woodfull
18. Kennington Oval
19. The MCC Waterford Crystal trophy
20. Billy Midwinter

ATHLETICS

1. Carl Lewis
2. General Ayub Khan
3. Alan Turing

4. Because it was wind-assisted
5. An advertisement
6. Sergey Bubka
7. P.T. Usha
8. Metal Ball
9. Usain Bolt
10. Hammer throw
11. High jump
12. The Russian athletics team was banned after the discovery of state-sponsored doping programme.
13. 50 km race walk
14. Triple jump
15. Stadium race
16. Marathon
17. Florence Griffith Joyner
18. Deepa Malik
19. Hima Das
20. Jesse Owens

BADMINTON

1. Poona
2. Carolina Marin
3. Leena Chandavarkar-Jeetendra
4. Syed Modi
5. Prakash Padukone
6. Goose
7. Sudirman Cup
8. One
9. Black
10. Herbert Scheele Trophy
11. All England Open

12. Asia
13. The country estate of the dukes of Beaufort
14. Lin Dan
15. P.V. Sindhu
16. Drop shot
17. Barcelona
18. 3 games of 21 points
19. Wood shot
20. *Playing to Win, My Life On and Off Court*

BOARD GAMES

1. Monopoly
2. Scrabble
3. Jigsaw puzzle
4. Akbar
5. Munshi Premchand
6. Cluedo
7. Snakes & Ladders
8. Risk
9. Trivial Pursuit
10. Twister
11. Ludo
12. Chinese Checkers
13. Backgammon
14. Pictionary
15. Othello
16. 81
17. Nine Men's Morris
18. Korean origin
19. Muzjiks
20. Scotland Yard

BOXING AND WRESTLING

1. K.D. Jadhav
2. Mike Tyson
3. Dohyo
4. Abraham Lincoln
5. Sakshi Malik
6. Joe Frazier
7. M.C. Mary Kom
8. Featherweight
9. The Rumble in the Jungle
10. Evander Holyfield
11. Napoleon Bonaparte
12. Sushil Kumar
13. Fireman's carry
14. John Sholto Douglas
15. White
16. Pugilism
17. Vijender Singh
18. Leon Spinks
19. France
20. Imagination

CARD GAMES

1. King of Hearts
2. A hand with no card above a nine
3. Canfield
4. A month of the year
5. Whist
6. Coins, cups and swords
7. Amitabh Bachchan
8. Germany

9. The Joker
10. Nine of diamonds
11. Gin rummy
12. Contract bridge
13. Eagles
14. *Alice's Adventures in Wonderland*
15. Liberties, equalities and fraternities
16. Ace of Spades
17. 21
18. Alexander Pushkin
19. *Great Expectations*
20. *The Sting*

ENTERTAINMENT AND SPORTS

1. Leander Paes
2. Milkha Singh
3. *Dangal*
4. *Chariots of Fire*
5. Ice Hockey
6. Sharmila Tagore
7. Sunil Gavaskar
8. *Moneyball*
9. Rugby
10. Gurinder Chadha
11. Angelina Jolie
12. Rocky Balboa
13. *Raging Bull*
14. *Million Dollar Baby*
15. *Any Given Sunday*
16. *Escape to Victory*
17. *Lagaan*

18. Bruce Lee
19. *Blades of Glory*
20. Muhammad Ali

FORMULA 1

1. The halo
2. There is danger ahead and you need to slow down.
3. Niki Lauda
4. Ayrton Senna
5. Jordan
6. Buddh International Circuit
7. Alfa Romeo
8. Hans Heyer
9. Michael Schumacher
10. Gilles and Jacques Villeneuve
11. Silverstone
12. Max Verstappen
13. Lella Lombardi
14. DRS
15. Undercutting
16. Not be allowed to start the race
17. Chicane
18. The Pit Wall
19. Kimi Raikkonen
20. Brawn GP

FIFA WORLD CUP

1. The match between Argentina and England in the 1986 FIFA World Cup in which Maradona led his side to victory.
2. Uruguay

3. Brazil
4. Alcides Ghiggia
5. Italy
6. Essam El Hadary
7. Score a golden goal
8. Playing with shoes
9. One place is reserved for the host nation.
10. Tunisia
11. Rinus Michels
12. Iceland
13. South America
14. Mexico
15. Pelī
16. Brazil
17. 1974 FIFA World Cup
18. 1970
19. Michel Platini
20. Just Fontaine

FOOTBALL

1. Johan Cruyff
2. Lothar Herbert Matthaeus
3. Cristiano Ronaldo
4. Luis Suarez
5. Garrincha
6. Arsenal
7. Arsene Wenger
8. Spain
9. UEFA Champions League
10. Juventus
11. Lionel Messi

12. Michael Jordan, his hero, wore it for the Chicago Bulls
13. George Best
14. Mahatma Gandhi
15. Durand Cup
16. Neville D'Souza
17. Manchester City
18. Cristiano Ronaldo
19. Sir Alex Ferguson
20. Sunil Chhetri

GOLF

1. Jack Nicklaus
2. Gene Sarazen
3. Green jacket of Augusta
4. S.S.P. Chawrasia
5. Ben Hogan
6. Tiger Woods
7. Albatross
8. To protest against Apartheid
9. A belt
10. Woodrow Wilson
11. Fiji
12. Babe Didrikson Zaharias
13. Arthur Conan Doyle
14. Caddy
15. Tee
16. The ball. The ball should have a maximum weight of 1.62 ounces (45.93 grams) and a minimum diameter of 1.62 inches (4.11 cm).
17. Calcutta
18. Alan Shepard

19. Treaty of Glasgow
20. Arnold Palmer

HOCKEY

1. Shepherd's crook
2. Artificial turf
3. Balbir Singh Sr.
4. M.S. Dhoni
5. Puck
6. It has produced more than 8 Olympians for India
7. Great Britain
8. Malaysia
9. Wayne Gretzky
10. Udham Singh and Leslie Claudius
11. Mumbai
12. Beighton Cup
13. Golden Whistle
14. He was the captain
15. Vidya Sharma
16. Kookaburras
17. Roop Singh
18. Jay Stacy
19. Donald Bradman
20. He designed the trophy of the Hockey World Cup.

INDIGENOUS GAMES

1. Kerala
2. Ashtamudi Lake
3. Polo
4. Jallikattu
5. Kho-kho

6. Mallakhamb
7. Wrestling
8. Langdi
9. Dhop Khel
10. Silambam
11. coconuts and a bunch of plantains
12. Gatka
13. Stick fighting
14. Coconut
15. Akhara
16. Punjab
17. Boat race
18. Ahmedabad
19. Kabaddi
20. Archery

INDIAN PREMIER LEAGUE

1. Sachin Tendulkar
2. Brendon McCullum
3. The dates clashed with the Lok Sabha elections in India.
4. Arjuna Ranatunga
5. He was referred to as 'Ro-Hit' by Ravi Shastri.
6. M.S. Dhoni
7. Delhi Daredevils (renamed as Delhi Capitals)
8. Chennai Super Kings
9. Jos Buttler
10. Where talent meets opportunity
11. Play for six different teams
12. Mumbai Indians
13. Manish Pandey
14. Royal Challengers Bangalore

15. LED stumps
16. Chris Gayle
17. Sujoy Ghosh
18. Dwayne Bravo
19. Mumbai Indians
20. 4

MIXED BAG 1

1. Call Earvin Johnson Jr. 'Magic'
2. Archery
3. Fencing
4. UK
5. Shaquille O'Neal
6. Jack Hobbs
7. Viswanathan Anand
8. Jenga
9. Garry Kasparov
10. Beijing
11. Abhinav Bindra
12. Table tennis
13. Artistic gymnastics
14. Sherlock Holmes
15. Figure skating
16. Larry Bird
17. Le Bron James
18. Curling
19. Tennis
20. Tour de France

MIXED BAG 2

1. Cristiano Ronaldo

2. Sunil Gavaskar
3. Lacrosse
4. Breaststroke
5. Rowing
6. Volleyball
7. His sneakers
8. Pankaj Advani. He was awarded for billiards and snooker.
9. Michael Phelps
10. Judo
11. Alpine skiing
12. Athlete
13. Rugby
14. Bob Dylan
15. Basketball
16. Switzerland
17. Pierre de Coubertin
18. Table Tennis
19. Sledge
20. Tae kwon do

MIXED BAG 3

1. Duleepsinhji
2. Croquet
3. Bob Dylan
4. He designed the new trophy.
5. Lothar Herbert Matthaeus
6. The batsman was given 'not out'.
7. Larissa Latynina
8. Dhyan Chand
9. Charlie Sifford

10. 42
11. Monopoly
12. Robert Vince
13. Javelin throw
14. Edouard Manet
15. Wilfred Rhodes
16. Seven points
17. Rocky
18. Nadia's Theme
19. Lion
20. Jack Hobbs

OLYMPIC GAMES

1. All participating countries sent female athletes.
2. The Olympic motto
3. In front of the royal box in the stadium
4. Baron Pierre de Coubertin
5. For allegedly stealing a flag from the Japanese Imperial Palace
6. Greece
7. Michael Phelps
8. Golf
9. Equestrian
10. Emperor Nero
11. Gold, silver and bronze medals were awarded
12. Tokyo. Tokyo hosted the Asian Games in 1958 and the Summer Olympic Games in 1964.
13. Abebe Bikila
14. Freestyle skiing
15. Nadia Comaneci
16. Syria

17. Wrestling
18. Netherlands
19. Abhinav Bindra
20. Painting

ONE DAY INTERNATIONAL AND THE WORLD CUP

1. 40
2. To raise awareness about breast cancer.
3. Ricky Ponting
4. They have represented two countries in ODIs.
5. Hit six sixes in an over
6. Mohinder Amarnath
7. Don Bradman
8. Shoaib Akthar
9. Sachin Tendulkar
10. Shoaib Malik
11. Anil Kumble
12. Geoffrey Boycott
13. Jhulan Goswami
14. Virat Kohli
15. Peter Kirsten
16. Sourav Ganguly
17. Lasith Malinga
18. Aaqib Javed
19. M.S. Dhoni
20. Zero

SPORTS AND ANIMALS

1. Goat dragging
2. Polo
3. Football

4. Paul the Octopus
5. Jules Rimet Trophy
6. Get a mention in the Wisden Cricketers' Almanack
7. Qutb ud Din Aibak
8. Training
9. Alexander Fleming
10. Steeplechasing
11. Dog
12. Seabiscuit: An American Legend
13. Duck
14. Skijoring
15. Canada and USA
16. Bird scarer at Wimbledon
17. Buzkashi
18. Chariot race
19. Cockfighting
20. Falconry

TENNIS

1. Andre Agassi. The name of the autobiography is *Open*.
2. Billie Jean King
3. Ramanathan Krishnan
4. Bunny Austin
5. Sania Mirza
6. Tiebreak
7. Leander Paes
8. Roger Federer
9. John McEnroe
10. Rudyard Kipling
11. US Open
12. Steffi Graf

13. Martina Navratilova
14. Egg
15. Roger Federer
16. A player who has won the French Open and Wimbledon back-to-back.
17. Martina Hingis (after Martina Navratilova)
18. Henry V
19. Australia
20. It was more visible to television viewers.

TEST CRICKET

1. Prison rods of the cells of the two leaders
2. Pink
3. Charles Bannerman
4. Vinoo Mankad
5. Gordon Greenidge
6. Anil Dalpat
7. Pakistan
8. Chris Gayle
9. Cheteshwar Pujara
10. Lala Amarnath
11. Brian Lara
12. W.G. Grace
13. Irfan Pathan
14. Grant and Andy Flower
15. Karun Nair
16. England
17. South Africa
18. Iftikhar Ali Khan Pataudi
19. Mark Boucher
20. Lost ball